W9-ATT-985

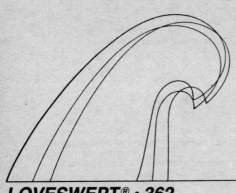

LOVESWEPT® • 362

Janet Evanovich
Back to the Bedroom

BANTAM BOOKS
NEW YORK • TORONTO • LONDON • SYDNEY • AUCKLAND

BACK TO THE BEDROOM
A Bantam Book / November 1989

LOVESWEPT® and the wave device are registered
trademarks of Bantam Books, a division of
Bantam Doubleday Dell Publishing Group, Inc.
Registered in U.S. Patent
and Trademark Office and elsewhere.

If you would be interested in receiving protective vinyl
covers for your Loveswept books, please write to this address
for information:

Loveswept
Bantam Books
P.O. Box 985
Hicksville, NY 11802

ISBN 0-553-22040-3

Published simultaneously in the United States and Canada

Bantam Books are published by Bantam Books, a division
of Bantam Doubleday Dell Publishing Group, Inc. Its trademark, consisting of the words "Bantam Books" and the
portrayal of a rooster, is Registered in U.S. Patent and
Trademark Office and in other countries. Marca Registrada.
Bantam Books, 666 Fifth Avenue, New York, New York 10103.

PRINTED IN THE UNITED STATES OF AMERICA

O   0 9 8 7 6 5 4 3 2 1

One

There were seven row houses on the 400 block of A Street NE. Six of them were Federal style: narrow three-story red brick buildings with long, arched windows and flat roofs. Each had a small false front peak imprinted with the date of construction—1881, 1884, or 1878. As was the custom at that time, basements were accessible from the front, five steps down. The first floor was five steps up. Front doors were sunk into arched alcoves, and the doors were thick oak, capped by decorative lead windows. Yards were small, minuscule actually, but packed with flowers, herbs, ivies, and stunted dogwood trees. The residents of A Street NE used every available inch in their tiny yards just as they filled every available second in their busy lives. It was a carefully restored Capitol Hill neighborhood with inflated Washington property values. And it was inhabited by ambitious professionals. The street wasn't so wide or so heavily traveled that it couldn't be crossed to say hello. Old-fashioned globed streetlights studded the narrow margin between curb and red brick sidewalk, casting circles of light on shiny BMWs, Jaguar sedans, VW convertibles, and Saab 900s.

In the middle of the block, flanked on either side by its tall, dark, dignified Federal neighbors, sat a fat two-story Victorian town house. Its brick had been painted pale, pale gray, the elaborate ribbon and bow stucco trim was gleaming white, and its gray tile mansard roof was steeply slanted. The house was dominated by a rounded half-turret facade with a conical gray tile roof tipped in silver and topped with a flying horse weather vane. It was an outrageous house, a birthday cake in a showcase filled with bran muffins. And it was inhabited by David Peter Dodd, who at first glance was neither birthday cake, nor bran muffin, nor A Street material by any stretch of the imagination. With his brown hair, brown eyes, medium build, and average height, he wasn't a man you would immediately notice, and he preferred it that way. He was thirty-one but he looked younger, and he was sitting on the front stoop of his house reading a G.I. Joe comic book when a large object fell from the sky and crashed through the roof of his next door neighbor's house.

Katherine Finn, called Kate to her face and the Formidable Finn behind her back, was in her kitchen when she heard the crash. It sounded more like an explosion than an intrusion. The overhead Casablanca fan jiggled from the vibration, windows rattled, and a bedraggled hanging Boston fern broke from its moorings and smashed onto the kitchen floor. The half-empty quart of milk Kate was holding slid from her fingers. She felt her heart jump to her throat, muttered an expletive, and ran to the front door, pausing in mid-stride when the house settled down to eerie silence. She stood absolutely still for a moment, listening, but she was unable to hear anything over the pounding of her heart. When her pulse rate slowed back to a normal beat, allowing her some semblance of rational thought, she concluded if anything were liable to explode, it would have to be in the cellar. There were things down there that made odd rumbling noises when they were working. There were pilot lights and emergency off-on switches and an intimidating tangle of pipes and wires. She took a deep breath, opened the cellar door, and sniffed. No smoke. She switched on the light and crept down the stairs. No fire. No evidence of explosion. She shook her head in confusion and turned to go back upstairs.

And let out a shriek when she bumped into David Dodd.

He looked at her over his large tortoiseshell glasses and reached out to steady her. "Are you okay?"

She clapped her hand to her heart and gasped for breath. "You scared me!"

"I heard the noise, and I came to see if you were all right. The door was open. . . ." He made a vague gesture in that direction and removed his glasses. They'd been neighbors for three months, but he'd never been in her house before. In fact, he'd never spoken more than three words to her at any one time. But that hadn't stopped him from forming an opinion. He'd observed that she was a woman who moved fast and kept erratic hours. She didn't dally between her car and her front door, barely taking time to wave and mumble "hello" while she fumbled for keys. She usually rushed by him in a stern black coat that hung almost to her ankles with a huge leather purse slung over her shoulder, a grocery bag balanced on her hip, plastic-draped clothes from the cleaners caught in the crook of a finger, and more often than not, she was dragging a large, odd-shaped metal case that was equipped with casters and stamped with a bunch of travel stickers. Because he didn't know her name, Dodd thought of her as the Mystery Woman. He was fascinated by the amount of raw energy she exuded between curb and door-step. Her impersonal, hurried hellos annoyed the hell out of him. And he hated the damn black coat.

Dave knew he was in big trouble when he started hating the coat. It was just a piece of clothing, for crying out loud. It belonged to a woman who was a virtual stranger. So what if the coat was unflattering? So what if it was missing a button on the half belt at the small of her back? It was none of his business, right? Wrong. It was driving him nuts. Clearly it was the result of having too much free time on his hands, Dave thought. He was getting weird. He had become fixated on a neighbor who wanted nothing to do with him. He'd been lonely, and wondered if she were lonely too. And then he started wondering what was under the all-concealing coat. A tweed suit? A silky dress? Maybe nothing at all?

Now he was finally standing next to the Mystery Woman, and his heart was pounding. Normal reaction when worrying about the safety of a neighbor, he told himself. It had nothing to with the fact that her complexion was flawless, or that she had outrageous Little Orphan Annie hair. She was smaller than he'd originally thought. About five feet five and delicately boned with a pixieish face and large green eyes. She was wearing a pair of baggy gray sweats that molded to her soft curves and clung to her small waist. David concentrated on her blue and gray running shoes while he tried to exert some control over his hormones.

She took a step backward and swiped at the wispy curls that fell across her forehead. "I don't understand it. Everything seems to be okay here."

"I guess it didn't make it to the cellar."

She looked at him sideways. "What are you talking about?"

"The thing that crashed through your roof. It must have stopped on the second floor."

Her eyes opened wide. "Something crashed through my roof? I thought it was an explosion in my cellar."

David took her elbow and nudged her toward the stairs. "I think the only thing that exploded was your milk. It's all over your kitchen floor."

"Okay, wait a minute, let me get this straight. You saw something crash through my roof. As in 'dropped from the sky' kind of crashed through my roof?"

"I didn't actually see it so much as hear it. There was a helicopter. I remember it making those *whump, whump, whump* sounds, and then . . ." He made a whistling sound through his teeth and ended with an explosion. "Right through your roof," he concluded.

Kate pushed him aside and took the stairs two at a time. The house was only one room wide. The front door opened to a foyer, which led to the small living room. An elaborate mahogany arch separated it from the dining room, and the kitchen, surprisingly large, was at the back of the house. There were two bedrooms and a bath upstairs. Kate halted abruptly at the door to the front bedroom and gasped. Splintered beams and roofing material hung crazily from a ragged hole in the ceiling, chunks of plaster were strewn about the room, sunlight poured through the roof, and a mist of fine powder floated in the air like fairy dust. The queen-size bed was collapsed in on itself, and square in the middle of it rested a scarred chunk of twisted metal. "My Lord, what is it?"

David approached it cautiously. "I'm not sure, but I think it's a camera pod from the helicopter. I used to do a lot of photography. Once I did an aerial survey for a new subdivision in Fairfax County, and we had an auxiliary video camera mounted on a pod like this.

Kate felt dazed. A helicopter part had fallen through

her roof. It made perfect sense. That was the sort of week she was having. On Wednesday her accountant had called to say her taxes were being audited. She'd gotten a speeding ticket on Thursday and a parking ticket on Friday. And this morning the cleaners had informed her of a "small mishap" to her favorite black coat. It was all too much even for Katherine Finn, a master at defusing frustration. She was a professional musician, a child prodigy who'd begun auditioning at the age of seven. By the time she was twelve she'd suffered more stress, humiliation, and rejection than most people do in a lifetime . . . and she'd also reaped more rewards and more successes. She didn't have a temperamental or mean bone in her entire body, but early on she'd learned how to manipulate, how to protect her ego, how to throw a well-aimed temper tantrum. Katherine Finn would never have a heart attack from suppressing emotion. Katherine Finn smashed plates, hugged babies, devoured food, and cried buckets at weddings, funerals, and sad movies. "Do you know what this used to be?" she shouted at David Dodd as she furiously paced beside the bed. "This used to be a brand-new three-hundred-dollar feather quilt. Prime goose down that was going to keep me warm this winter."

David raised his eyebrows and looked at the quilt with obvious envy.

"I suppose you think goose down grows on trees. Well, let me tell you, I worked long and hard for that stupid goose down. And now what? Who's going to pay for this " She paused and ran a hand through her hair. "I should call someone," she said. "My insurance company, the police, the airport. Bloomingdale's linen department." She looked up at the swatch of blue sky showing through her roof. "I need a carpenter, a roofer. Damn, it's Saturday. I'll never be able to get a carpenter out here today. What if it rains? What if word gets around about this? Degenerates and drug addicts could just drop in whenever they wanted." She narrowed her eyes and shifted from foot to foot. "Boy, I'd just like to see them try. I'd be on them like white on rice."

David believed her. She had that tight-lipped don't-mess-with-me look a Doberman gets when he hasn't eaten in three days. Her eyes were a flash of emerald green. Her hair seemed electric. She was getting hysterical, he decided. And she was magnificent. He picked up the bedside phone and dialed.

"Who are you calling?" Kate asked. "The police?"

"No, the pizza place on the corner. You look like you could use lunch." For the life of him, David couldn't figure out why he wanted to feed this crazy person. Common decency, he told himself. He shook his head. That was a bunch of bull. He wasn't all that decent. He silently groaned and grimly acknowledged that he was hooked. Now that he knew what was under the awful black coat, there was no turning back. Now he wanted to get rid of the gray sweats. He wanted to get rid of them *bad*.

Kate looked at the man standing in her bedroom and realized she didn't know his name. Although he'd moved in three months earlier, she'd never introduced herself. She was a lousy neighbor. She probably should have baked him a cake or something. She'd practically snubbed him, and he'd still rushed over to help her when disaster struck. A nice person, she thought. And he was ordering pizza! A little offbeat, but thoughtful. "Is pizza your standard remedy for hysterical women?"

He had his hands plunged into the pockets of faded jeans that had a hole worn through at the knee, a blue and black plaid flannel shirt draped loose over a navy T-shirt, and he was standing back on his heels in new white tennis shoes, watching her. "No, but I thought it might be too soon for brandy."

"You mean too early."

"Mmmm. Too early."

Not only didn't she know his name, but she wasn't sure if he was married. She had never seen him go off to work, and she was surprised at how attractive he was. From a distance he'd seemed loose-jointed and boyish, but at close range he had a compact, muscular body. He was about five eleven with corded arms, a flat belly, and eyes that were a deep, rich brown. The eyes didn't miss much, and they didn't give away much, she decided. Nothing more than he wanted. They were intelligent and perceptive. He had a wide, firm mouth that looked a trifle stubborn but held a hint of humor. "I don't think we've actually met," she said, holding out her hand. "Katherine Finn. Everyone calls me Kate."

"David Dodd."

"I've been a crummy neighbor."

"Yup."

Kate raised her nose a fraction of an inch. It was an intimidating gesture she used when put on the defensive: a habit developed after years of coping with four brothers and countless arrogant, eccentric music teachers.

Dave grinned at her. "Nice try, but haughty isn't going to work. You should have baked me a cake. Emily Pearson, across the street, baked me a cake. And Mrs. Butler, in the corner house, baked me a cake."

Kate controlled the impulse to make a face and say something rude about Emily Pearson and Mrs. Butler. They were nice people. And they made her crazy. Their windows were always spotless. They put up appropriate door ornaments for Halloween, Thanksgiving, and Christmas. They baked fruit cakes for neighbors and made chicken soup for sick people. For a woman who once left her Christmas lights up until July and didn't own a pie plate, they were a hard act to follow. "I was going to bake you a cake, but I just never got around to it."

"It's not too late. You could bake me a cake today."

"Don't get pushy."

The grin widened. "Just trying to be helpful. I didn't want you to carry around a load of unnecessary guilt."

"Very thoughtful of you. The truth is, I'm not much of a baker."

He slung his arm around her shoulder and guided her out of the bedroom, down the stairs. "Hey, you can't let that stop you. Baking isn't so tough. I happen to have a no-fail layer cake recipe that'll knock your socks off. Since you're obviously not the domestic type, I'll make the cake and—"

Kate dug her heels into the runner. "Hold it," she said, hands on hips. "What do you mean, obviously not the domestic type?"

"Domestic types always know how to bake cakes." He stood at the foot of the stairs and looked around at the bare living room and dining room. "And domestic types usually own furniture."

Kate followed his gaze around the two rooms. "I'm divorced. He got the furniture, and I got the house payments." As she appraised the empty living room, she pushed her hair behind her ears, but it immediately sprang forward to its original position. "I suppose I could use a chair or something, but I haven't much money left over at the end of the month." She seemed lost in her own thoughts for a moment while she remembered how the house had looked filled with Anatol's furniture. Sleek black leather and gleaming chrome stuff that she'd hated. "Of course, it's easier to vacuum this way," she concluded.

"I'm sorry about your divorce."

She made a dismissive gesture. "We're still friends. We just weren't destined to live together. We drove each other crazy. The divorce didn't signify failure, but a truce."

He reached out and wrapped a red curl around his finger. "So you're hard to live with, huh?"

Kate whisked the curl away with a snap of her head. "I'm impossible."

"I'm easy to live with," he announced as he followed her into the kitchen. "I'm very likable."

She raised her eyebrows. He was likable all right. He was so likable it was frightening. She felt mildly threatened, thoroughly intrigued, and uncomfortably attracted to him. She'd never been skydiving, but she thought it must feel like this. Accelerated heart rate, light stomach, rush of adrenaline, heady exhilaration and at the same time a grim determination not to crash and die.

He took a cookie from the open bag on the kitchen counter. "Don't you think I'm likable?" He knew he was likable. He'd made a whole career out of being invisible and likable. It was a natural talent.

"You sound a little cynical about it."

He munched on the cookie, surprised that the cynicism had crept out. "It's a curse."

"Uh-huh." Kate dropped a kitchen towel onto the floor and sopped up the milk. "You want to call the police or you want to clean the floor?"

He reached for the wall phone. "No contest."

An hour later, after finishing their pizza, they led an FAA investigator up to the bedroom. "So," Kate said hopefully, "anyone report a missing piece of metal?"

The man paled and swore softly at the wreckage. "I'm glad you're not a late sleeper." He photographed the ceiling and the bed and returned with a packing crate. "We'll be in touch as soon as we get this straightened out."

A respresentative from her insurance company arrived fifteen minutes later. "Heard on the weather report that it's supposed to rain," he said, looking at the hole in Kate's roof. "Supposed to get colder too."

Kate peered up at the patch of sky showing through her ceiling and groaned. It really wasn't fair that misfortune had singled her out. She wasn't such a bad person, she thought. A little disorganized and maybe just a teensy bit self-centered. So she wasn't such a great neighbor, but hey, she'd been busy. And it wasn't as if she'd been an *awful* neighbor. She was quiet most of the time, and she usually parked in her own parking space, and she almost always said hello to him. . . .

The alarm rang on her bedside clock. Simultaneously, an alarm went off in the kitchen. Kate smacked her forehead with the heel of her hand. "Oh, damn!"

Dave reached for the clock. "What's going on?"

"I'm late!" Kate rushed to her closet and grabbed a garment bag. "That's my late alarm. I'm awful with time. When the alarms go off it means I have only half an hour to get to the Kennedy Center and dress. Special matinee today. I knew I'd forget!" She snagged her big leather purse from the dresser and took off at a dead run. She got halfway down the stairs, turned, and popped back into the bedroom. "Dave, can you take care of this for me? And lock up the house when you leave. And thanks for the pizza."

She was gone. Dave and the insurance man stared out the open bedroom door in silence, unconsciously holding their breath. They resumed breathing at the sound of a car being gunned from the curb.

The insurance man blinked and smiled in amazement. "Is she always like this?"

"Probably."

By the time Kate returned, it was pouring. She dashed from her car and huddled in the dark alcove of her front door, searching through her purse for her key. The concert had been followed by a mandatory reception and dinner that had seemed interminable. She'd cracked her knuckles when the consommé was served, tapped her foot relentlessly through the chicken almondine, and bolted down her poached pear in raspberry sauce. When rain had softly pattered against the windows, a variety of emotions had run through her. She'd been relieved that it wasn't a good night for rapists to go prowling around looking for houses with holes in their roofs, concerned that, in addition to everything else, she now had water damage—and an undeniable yearning for David Dodd's no-fail layer cake. She shivered now as rain drizzled down her neck and soaked into the back of her sweats and wistfully longed for the black coat the cleaner had destroyed. The coat had been like Little Bear's porridge. Not too hot, and not too cold. It had always been just right. Not too long, not too short. It had fit her perfectly. And now it was gone . . . just like her roof. Damn. She wedged her music case between her leg and the door, protecting it from the elements out of habit. She found the key and let herself into the foyer, for the first time in her life feeling slightly insecure in her own house. Her haven, her sanctum santorum was vulnerable. It had been violated by a pod. Whatever that was. "A pod!" she said aloud. "A big, stupid pod." She shook the rain from her hair and apprehensively trudged upstairs, hating the feeling of doom that had descended on her since she'd entered the house. *Don't get paranoid about this*, she told herself. It was one of those once-in-a-lifetime freak accidents, and now that she'd gotten it out of the way, the coast was clear. She was in good shape for the next hundred years. Still, it was creepy to have something drop out of the sky into your bed.

She switched the light on in her bedroom and pressed her lips together at the sight of the quilt. It was dead. It smelled like wet fowl, and water dripped from the ceiling with a depressing *splat* onto the soggy lump of torn coverlet and massacred feathers. Something thumped overhead. Footsteps on her roof. The sound of a heavy object being dragged toward her. She swallowed and clapped her hand over her mouth. The rapists had found her! She searched for a weapon. Hairbrush, flannel nightgown, empty yogurt cup. In desperation her hand closed around a cut-glass perfume atomizer. "Whoever's up on my roof better not come any closer." She aimed the atomizer at the hole. "I've got Mace."

David Dodd peeked over the edge and grinned down at her. "That's not Mace. That's a perfume atomizer. The best you could do with that is strip me of my masculine body odor."

"You have to use your imagination."

"Un-huh."

She squinted into the darkness of the third floor. "What are you doing up there?"

"Trying to fix your roof. I'd have had it fixed sooner, but I had to drive all over town trying to find a big enough piece of plastic." He disappeared and a slab of wooden slats was shoved halfway across the opening.

Kate recognized it as a section of the six-foot-high privacy fence that divided their backyards.

"Hope you don't mind that I used part of the fence," he said, inching it into place. "It's hard to get a lumber delivery on Saturday night." He walked around the perimeter of the hole and reached forward to tug the wood into place. Then there was the sound of tarred paper tearing and David Dodd dropped like a stone, through the roof, through the second floor ceiling and landed with a *whump* that knocked the air out of him, flat on his back, spread-eagle on the soaking wet, smashed-in bed.

Two

Kate was afraid he was dead. He lay motionless on the bed, eyes closed, his body encased in a yellow slicker, his hands limp in small pools of gray feather water. She felt the breath clog in her throat, felt anguish smothering clear thought. "Lord, no!" she whispered, rushing to his side, acting on instinct, never noticing the wet mattress she crawled across. She straddled his inert form, tugged at the raincoat zipper, and put her hand to his heart. *"Dave!"*

He opened his eyes. "Mmm?"

She almost collapsed in relief. "Thank God. I thought you were dead."

If he were dead, then this had to be heaven, because the Mystery Woman was sitting astride him, her warm hand pressed against his chest, her nifty butt resting on his thighs. Black dots floated in front of his eyes, and he struggled to regulate his breathing.

Kate leaned closer. "Your heart is racing under my hand."

He gritted his teeth and thought that was nothing compared to what was happening under the center seam of her sweat pants. He firmly grabbed her and lifted her up, leaving wet handprints on the sleeves of her shirt. "I'm okay. I was just stunned for a minute." He sat up slowly, flexing his arms and legs, amazed that nothing seemed broken. Tomorrow he'd probably feel like a truck had run over him. Rain drizzled onto the top of his head and dripped off the tip of his nose. He set his mouth in a grim line and narrowed his eyes. "Outta my way, woman. I've got a score to settle with this roof."

"You're not going back up there. . . ."

"Damn right I'm going back up there. Hell, us hero types don't let a little thing like a broken back stop us. When there's a damsel in distress, we go for it. Grab the gusto, full speed ahead, man the torpedos."

Kate followed him up to the third floor and unlocked the trapdoor to the roof. "Be careful!"

His face lit up. "Would you care if I got hurt?"

"Of course I'd care. I mean, you're my neighbor."

"Uh-huh."

"And, uh, you're a nice person."

"That's true." He leaned toward her. "Anything else?"

Kate pushed the bangs back from her forehead,

shifted from foot to foot, and considered kissing him. He had a terrific voice, she thought. It had turned deep and rumbly . . . very sexy, very comfortable, very intimate. The sort of voice that made her feel as if she'd known him for a thousand years. The sort of voice that said that as far as he was concerned, she was the only woman on the face of the earth. And his eyes confirmed it. They were frankly admiring and slightly predatory. "Do you live alone?"

"Yup."

"Not married?"

"Nope."

"Engaged?"

"Nope."

"You aren't gay, are you?"

His mouth curved at the corners. "No. Want me to take a blood test?"

"Maybe later."

The husky resonance returned to his voice. "That sounds promising."

"You shouldn't get your hopes up. I'm impulsive and emotional—about everything but sex."

"Sex is serious stuff, huh?"

"You bet."

"Good. I'm a serious kind of guy."

Kate smiled. "I know. I could tell that from the literature you select for yourself. You ever read anything besides *G.I. Joe?*"

"*Spider-Man.*"

"Is that how you got up on my roof just now? Spider-Man techniques?"

"Our roofs are joined together. I walked from mine to yours." He sighed. "Speaking of roofs . . ." He put his foot on the bottom rung of the swing-down stairs. "If I fall through your ceiling again, feel free to stimulate me back to life."

"You mean like cold water, a slap on the face?"

"I was thinking more along the lines of mouth-to-mouth, loosening my clothes . . ."

Kate watched him disappear into the darkness and decided he was a little outrageous. She liked that. She was outrageous too. Outrageous felt comfortable to her. "What are you doing out there?" she yelled. "Are you okay?"

"Yeah. I've got the fence in place. Now all I have to do is cover it with the plastic and put a few bricks around to hold everything down."

The third floor of Kate's house was nothing more than a stairwell and one huge room. Sound echoed off the curtainless windows and hardwood floors, and light from the bedroom below splashed in crazy patterns against the bare walls. "This is not a pleasant sight," Kate said when Dave returned. "This is . . . horrible. Like in horror-movie horrible. And my bedroom is even more depressing."

Dave watched water drip from the edge of his slicker onto his shoes. "I need to get dry. And you need to cheer up. How about we both go over to my house for a while."

"I don't know. I feel sort of guilty about leaving my sinking ship."

He nudged her down the stairs toward the front

door. "Your ship isn't sinking. And it won't mind being left alone. Trust me. I know about these things."

"Oh, yeah? How do you know?"

"I've been left alone and I never minded."

Kate raised an eyebrow. "Never?"

"Almost never. Actually, I hated it, but that's because I'm a person, and this is a house, and I don't think houses mind so much. I suppose you don't own a raincoat."

"No. I had this really great black coat, but it got ruined at the cleaners today. I used to have an umbrella somewhere. . . ."

The coat was ruined. What a shame. Dave could hardly keep the smile from spreading across his face. He took his slicker off and wrapped it around her. "Just make a dash for it. My door's unlocked."

His house was almost as narrow as hers, but its mood was entirely different. Two forest-green wing chairs filled the alcove created by the half-turret facade. A large overstuffed plaid couch had been placed across from the chairs, and a dented copper milk-jug lamp cast warm light around the front room. Embers of a dying fire glowed in the small black marble fireplace. Kate closed her eyes and inhaled. Charred applewood and fresh-baked spice cake. "Every house in America should smell like this," she said. "This is Mom's apple pie."

"Actually, it's a generic box mix with two eggs and oil added."

Kate followed him to the kitchen at the back of the house and sniffed the layer cake cooling on wire racks on the counter. "This smells great. You baked this for me, didn't you?"

"Yeah. Are you impressed?"

She picked a crumb from the counter and nibbled it. "Absolutely. You fix roofs, you bake cakes, you feed pizza to distraught women." She watched him drop a handful of beans into a coffee grinder and add water to the electric coffee maker. "You grind your own coffee beans." She plopped into a ladder-back chair. "What else do you do?"

"That's about it."

"What sort of job do you have?"

"I'm . . . between jobs."

She'd never been between jobs. Music stretched like an invisible continuous thread weaving its way through the fabric of her life. Friends, houses, coats, and cars had come and gone, but her job was constant. Her job was to make music, and to make it perfectly wonderfully. The concept of a worthwhile person being between jobs was difficult for her to grasp. "Have you been between jobs for very long?"

"About six months." Bulldog, he thought grimly. He could see it in her eyes. She was going to sink her teeth into him and hang on until she had him figured out. He imagined she did that with music. She was probably a holy terror. "You're a musician?"

"Yup."

"What instrument?"

"Cello."

He flipped the cake onto a plate and handed Kate

a butter knife. "How about if you frost the cake while I take a shower."

A stab of panic raced through her stomach. "I don't know how to frost a cake."

"Do you know how to open a can?" He set a large can of chocolate frosting on the table next to the cake.

"Son of a gun." She smiled. "What will they think of next?"

He took the slicker from her and hung it on a wall hook. "Your sweats are wet at the cuffs and knees. I'll throw a dry pair down to you."

Kate nodded acknowledgment and peeled back the easy-open lid. "This is amazing," she said. "Look at this—frosting in a can." She took a big glob of brown gunk on the tip of her knife and swirled it across the cake. "I love it!"

Dave looked at her in amazement. "Haven't you ever been in a supermarket?"

"Sure. But I never thought to look for frosting in a can. I'm always in such a rush. When I was a kid all I did was practice, practice, practice. I guess my mom made cakes, but I never paid much attention. There weren't cooking facilities at the conservatory, and when I took up housekeeping with Anatole we had lots of money and bought ready-made cakes. We bought everything ready-made."

"What does this Anatole person do?"

"Plays the oboe. He's wonderful."

Dave raised an eyebrow. "Wonderful across the board? Or wonderful on the oboe?"

Kate slopped more frosting on the cake. "On the oboe. He's a genius. Of course I'm a genius too." She rubbed her nose with the back of her hand and left a smear of icing traveling down her cheek. "But I'm not as great a genius as Anatole."

Dave was developing a fast dislike for Anatole. Where'd he get off being a bigger genius than Kate? He wanted to make an insulting remark, but he stopped himself. He should think of an intelligent response. Something civilized. "Must have been hard having two geniuses living in the same house."

"It was bloody awful." She looked up at Dave with sudden insight. "You know, I didn't really mind the hysterics and the clashes in personality. I minded the loneliness. We were like ships passing in the night. Separate entities, never really touching, self-absorbed. And it wasn't any fun." Her face lit in a smile that took David Dodd's breath away. "Neither of us knew about frosting in a can."

"Guess there's all kind of genius," he said, feeling foolishly happy. His wet shoes squished water onto the kitchen linoleum and he wondered if anyone else felt the earth shift in its orbit. He still felt happy when he went to sleep that night.

Kate opened one eye and directed an oath at the person pounding on her front door. She snuggled deeper into the sleeping bag Dave had loaned her, but the pounding continued. She looked at her watch. Seven-thirty. What idiot was pounding on her door at seven-thirty in the morning? Didn't they know she was tired? Didn't they know she'd slept on the living room floor because it had the upgraded rug? The pounding stopped and was replaced by strange scuffling, scratching sounds on her small front porch. Kate sat up in the bag and watched a little old lady inch across the front window. The woman was standing spread-eagle on the wide outdoor window frame, clinging to the raised brickwork, and she was looking in at Kate. She reminded Kate of Piglet when the wind had picked him up and plastered him against Owl's treehouse window.

"I've come to see about the room you've advertised in the paper," she shouted through the glass, "but I'm not going to sleep on no floor. They make everybody sleep on the floor here?"

Kate unzipped the bag and padded barefoot to the foyer. It had stopped raining, and it had turned cold. The wind whipped through her flannel nightgown when she poked her head out the front door. "What are you doing on my window?"

"No one was answering the door, so I thought I'd get up here and take a look at the place."

Kate crept out onto the porch. "Well, here I am. I'm answering the door. You can get down now."

"No I can't. I can't get down."

"Wonderful. Okay, I'll try to give you a hand. Just hang on." Kate swung a leg over the wrought iron railing and grabbed the back of the old lady's coat. "Gotcha! Try to work your way over to me."

"I'm going to fall."

"No you're not. I've got hold of you."

"That's the problem, you ninny. You're pulling me off the ledge." Elsie reached out and grabbed a handful of nightgown in a last-ditch effort to keep her balance, but it was too late. A moment later both women were lying in a heap in an eighteen-year-old azalea bush.

David Dodd stood on the rain-splattered brick sidewalk with a bag of doughnuts in his hand. "If I hadn't seen this with my own eyes, I'd never have believed it."

Kate tugged her nightgown down over her knees and struggled to free herself from the bush. "Where'd you come from? Why do you always arrive *after* a disaster?"

"I went to the bakery. I always go to the bakery on Sunday morning." He lifted Kate off the flattened azalea. "I was walking down the street, thinking how boring my life was before I met you, and there you were . . . flying through the air in your nightgown."

"Ain't nobody gonna help me up?" Elsie asked. "I probably broke every bone in my body."

Dave eased her to her feet and plucked a twig from hair the color and texture of steel wool. "Next time you do windows you should use a ladder," he said.

Elsie narrowed her eyes at him. "I don't do windows. I'm here about the room." She straightened her coat, hauled herself up the front stairs, and let herself into the house. "How come there's no furniture in this house?"

"Easier to vacuum," Dave said.

"Hmmph, one of them clean freaks, huh? That's

okay by me, but I'm an old lady. I need a bed, a chair, a TV. I suppose the room's upstairs?"

"Yeah, but the room's sort of a mess," Kate said. "It's not really ready to be rented."

Elsie stuffed her hands onto her hips and leaned forward, all set for battle. "Say what, child? If it's not ready to be rented, then how come you advertised?"

"I had this little accident here yesterday."

"Uh-huh," Elsie said. "What kind of accident?"

"A chunk of metal from a helicopter fell through my roof."

"Uh-huh."

Kate brushed at a smudge of mud on her nightgown. "And it rained before we could close up the hole."

Elsie pressed her lips together and stomped up the stairs. "Chunk off a helicopter," she muttered. "Can you imagine? A helicopter." She stopped at Kate's bedroom door and looked at the bed. Then she looked at the ceiling. "It ain't so bad," she said. "I've seen worse. So where's my room?"

Kate's eyes traveled to the hole in the ceiling. "I was thinking of renting the third floor."

"I guess that'd be okay. You don't have loud goings-on in this bed, do you? I don't put up with that sort of thing."

"I don't have *any* goings-on in this bed."

Dave raised his eyebrows in a look that said, Oh, yeah? I could fix that.

Kate grabbed the bag of doughnuts, took a Boston

cream, and stuffed it into her mouth. "Eg wibe thad smile oaf your fash," she said, glaring at Dave.

Elsie had gone up to the third floor and was looking down at them through the hole. "Maybe we could cover this with a rug or something."

Kate swallowed a big lump of doughnut. "I need coffee."

"We're going downstairs to make coffee," Dave called to Elsie. "You want some?" He saw the horrified look on Kate's face and shrugged. "I like her."

"Coffee would hit the spot," Elsie said. "How many doughnuts have you got?"

"A whole bagful."

Elsie clomped down the stairs and held her hand out to Dave. "I guess I never introduced myself. Elsie Hawkins. You own this place? You always serve continental breakfast on Sunday?"

"David Dodd. Nope. I'm the next door neighbor. This is Katherine Finn. She owns the place."

"Shoot. Don't suppose you have a room to rent," she said to David.

"Afraid not."

"All right, then I guess I'm stuck here." She took Kate's hand and shook it vigorously. "It's a deal. I'll rent your third floor even though you're kinda dingy. And look at that nightgown. Honey, what's a sweet young thing like you doing in a big ugly nightgown like that. No wonder your bed ain't seen no action."

"This is my favorite nightgown. It's soft and warm and it has little lavender roses on it." Kate turned to Dave. "You think this nightgown's big and ugly?"

He answered without a moment's hesitation. He did what any intelligent man would do—he lied. "No. Not ugly at all. Not with you in it." That much was true, he thought. Kate Finn could make a garbage bag look good. Besides, the nightgown wasn't exactly ugly. It was just inappropriate. Kate's tousled hair and bottle-green eyes needed satin. A hot-pink satin nightshirt without panties. Or a slinky black silk teddy.

"Unh-unh, watch out for this one, child," Elsie said to Kate. "He's got plans."

That's when Kate decided Elsie Hawkins was okay. Elsie called it as she saw it, right up front. She'd pay her rent on time. She'd keep her room clean. And she wouldn't have a lot of parties. Anyone that honest couldn't have many friends.

"So what really happened here," Elsie said. "How'd you get that hole in your ceiling?"

Kate slid her feet into a pair of raccoon slippers and wrapped a furry pink bathrobe around herself. "I told you. It was part of a helicopter."

"Get out."

"Really."

Elsie took a doughnut from the bag. "So why did it fall on *your* roof?"

Kate belted the robe and went downstairs. "Guess I was just lucky."

"You sure it wasn't dropped on your house on purpose?"

"That's crazy." Her voice reflected more conviction than she actually felt. She couldn't think of a single person who would want to do such a thing, but she had to admit, it was a bizarre accident.

"Well, it seems kind of strange to me that a big old chunk of helicopter would all of a sudden drop off and fall through your roof. They check those things. They get out there and they kick those wheels before they take off. No sir, I bet this was no accident."

"The FAA is investigating," Kate said.

"Hah, a lot they'll find out. They'll come back and tell you they don't know whose plane it was. You wait and see. Remember last year when that little plane went down in northern Virginia? They said they couldn't identify the pilot. That's because he was a spy. Washington's crawling with spies." Elsie sat on a kitchen chair. She sat ramrod straight, her shiny black purse perched on the lap of the royal blue coat, her hands folded on top of the purse. "You aren't a spy, are you?" she asked Kate.

"Nope. I'm a cellist." She put a pot of water on the stove to boil and set a jar of instant coffee on the table. "Hope you don't mind instant. Anatole took the coffee maker."

Dave didn't mind instant as long as he could watch Kate move around the kitchen in her ridiculous fuzzy pink robe and outlandish raccoon slippers. Most of the women he knew would have rushed off to the bathroom to comb their hair and put on lipstick, but Kate obviously felt comfortable being rumpled. He liked that. She'd be the kind of woman who'd cuddle with you long into the night, not caring about wrinkled sheets or the tangles in her hair.

"I don't want you to get the wrong idea about this cup of coffee," Elsie said. "I'm not one of them kaffeeklatsch women. Don't expect me to be sociable like this all the time. I haven't got all day to sit around drinking coffee. I've got a job."

Kate pulled up a chair opposite her. "What kind of job?"

"I sling burgers at the Corner Café. Had to lie about my age because they'd think I was too old. I don't ordinarily hold with lying, but there are times when it feels damn good. No reason why a sixty-six-year-old woman can't sling burgers. I used to sell girdles in a specialty shop, but they retired me. Sold girdles for forty-two years. Just as well I was retired. I was sick of stuffing all those fat women into girdles and bras." She stirred her coffee, drank it down scalding hot, and stood to leave. "I gotta go now. Got a lot to do." She took a checkbook from her purse and stood at the kitchen counter while she filled in the blanks. "Here's two months rent," she said, handing the check to Kate. "Now all I need is my key."

Kate took a key from the hook over the toaster. "Here's the key, but the roof has a hole in it. . . ."

"I don't care about the roof. Last year when I retired I gave up my apartment and moved into a senior citizens' home. The place is driving me nuts. Nothing but old people in it. All they serve is food you don't have to chew. You ever see puréed beef? Looks like dog food." Elsie dropped her key into her purse. "I don't mind the hole in the roof. Looks like you patched it up okay. What I need is a bed without them dumb metal rails on the side."

Kate watched the front door close behind Elsie Hawkins. "Did that really happen?"

"I think you'd better hurry up and get a bed."

"It takes days, maybe weeks, to get a bed delivered."

"There's a big cash-and-carry store in Alexandria. You go get dressed, and I'll rent us a truck, and then we'll go buy some furniture."

Kate smiled at him. "I like the way you keep saying we."

"There's a price for my assistance." He reached out for her, but she moved away.

"Oh, yeah? What's the price?"

"Undying gratitude, friendship everlasting, a compliment once in a while. And I want to see what this silly robe feels like. What is this stuff? It looks like fake pink sheepskin."

"Yup. That's what it is. Fake pink sheepskin." She watched him warily. "This wouldn't just be a ploy to fondle me, would it?"

"Boy, that really hurt."

"Just checking."

"You get fondled a lot?"

"Almost never."

"I can believe that."

"Really?" Kate stuffed her hands into the pockets of her robe. "Is that an insult?"

"It's a compliment."

"Oh." Her face lit in a smile. "Thanks."

He reached out for her again—this time with more

success. He ruffled her hair and smoothed the collar of her bathrobe. "Soft."

"My robe?"

"Your hair. The robe is okay too." He was in love, he decided. Flat out in love. And he didn't know what to do about it. He jumped when an alarm went off. "Now what?"

"Damn." Kate whirled off to the kitchen and thumped her hand down on the clock. "I have a rehearsal. I belong to a chamber music group, and we have a performance this afternoon."

"You keep busy."

"This is nothing. I also give lessons. I coach a youth orchestra. I have performances four nights a week. And then I take exercise classes—"

"Sounds like a lot."

"Behind my back they call me the Formidable Finn. I'm a driven person."

Dave rocked back on his heels with his hands in his pockets. "Do you like that?"

"Of course I like it. Music is my life. I eat, sleep, and breathe music."

"Yeah, well, if you don't do something about a bed, you're going to be sleeping music on the floor again. With Elsie."

The upstairs alarm rang out and both of them grimaced.

"Damn! I hate that alarm," Kate shouted.

Dave sighed. "Listen, you go ahead to your rehearsal. I can take care of this bed stuff."

"That's really sweet of you, and I appreciate it—" She was already halfway up the stairs.

"But?"

"But it's not your problem. I'd feel like I was taking advantage of your friendship." She slammed the bedroom door. "I have to get dressed!"

He stood in the hallway and stared at the closed door. "So what are you going to do with Elsie?"

"She'll have to spend one more night in the old people's home." There was a full minute of silence. Kate opened the door. "On second thought . . ."

Dave grinned down at her. "You aren't afraid of Elsie, are you?"

"Of course I'm afraid of Elsie. Aren't you?"

"Maybe a little."

She was back in the gray sweats and powder-blue jogging shoes. "I'll be done in about two hours. We can go shopping then."

"What time's your concert?"

"Four," she shouted, going out the door. When she reached the bottom step, she turned around and ran back into the house.

"Forgot my cello!"

Three

They were on Route 395 heading north, driving past Crystal City, past the Pentagon on a road running parallel to the Potomac River. To the left Arlington National Cemetery sprawled in somber rows of white crosses with the Custis-Lee Mansion sitting high on a hill above. Dave kept to the right-hand lane and turned onto the Arlington Memorial Bridge. She looked at him expectantly when he parked on the corner of Constitution Avenue and Henry Bacon Drive. "I'm going to make a short stop over here. It'll only take a minute."

He pointed to a touch football game in progress on the playing field to their right. "See that group of guys? Those are the Blood-and-Guts Couch Potatoes. We play football every Sunday afternoon and basketball every Thursday night." He got out of the truck and jogged around to open the door for her.

"You belong to something called the Blood-and-Guts Couch Potatoes?"

He took her by the hand and pulled her along. "You bet. Charter member."

She curled her hand around his and thought it was interesting that from the very beginning, she'd never needed the usual amount of insulating body space with David Dodd. She liked being close to him. That was the problem; she liked it too much. And if the truth were known, she'd like to be even closer. A lot closer. She liked the way he held her hand, slid an arm around her shoulders, tweaked a curl. His touch was firm and confident without being grabby. It was possessive without being insulting. It was satisfying. David Dodd's touch filled a small corner of her that had been empty. Undoubtedly, it had something to do with the herding instinct, she decided. Animals needed physical contact. They needed to bump along together. And David Dodd was a good bumper. There was the potential for a wonderful friendship to grow between them. There was also the potential for a disastrous love affair. She shook off the latter thought. "Are you going to play football now?"

"No. I'm going to recruit someone to help us get the mattresses out of that sad excuse for a truck and up your stairs."

To Kate the Potatoes seemed like an unremarkable, rag-tag group of men dressed in mismatched sweats and ratty sneakers. Despite their name and their wide variety of ages, they looked like they were in okay shape. Someone pitched the ball to Dave, and he held on to it while the game was interrupted for introductions.

Dave waited a beat before slapping a cheerful smile onto his mouth. "So who's going to help me with these mattresses?"

None of the Potatoes looked too excited.

"Okay," Dave said, "beer and pizza."

Lenny Newfarmer retrieved his jacket from a pile lying on the ground. "Too cold to play today anyway," he said.

Another Potato admitted the sun was at the wrong angle and kept getting in his eyes. Smitty Smith thought it was too windy for football. Elmo Nichols shoes weren't fitting him just right, and Ron Miller had a cramp in his calf and doubted he could run much more.

Minutes later Kate buckled her seat belt and watched the men head to their cars. "Is there anything they won't do for beer and pizza?"

"Hey, we aren't named the Couch Potatoes for nothing."

"The Couch Potatoes looked like they were in pretty good shape."

"Yeah, we're into clean living."

As Dave drove down Constitution, he told her about the group. "Lenny Newfarmer and I used to work together. Elmo Nichols is military. He lives in the same apartment building as Lenny. I don't know where Smitty came from. He's Secret Service. Howard Berk, the guy in the Notre Dame sweatshirt is an economist at the World Bank. At least that's what he tells us. Smitty brought him into the group."

"Lenny Newfarmer is the short guy, right? The guy who was cold? The guy who was wearing two different colored socks?"

"That's him."

"You worked with him?"

"Yup."

"He looks like a street person."

Dave grinned. "He's a little eccentric."

"Don't suppose you want to tell me what you two did for a living?"

"Photography. Lenny's a terrific person but a terrible photographer. We were business partners for a while. It was a disaster."

"Photography business?"

"Mostly weddings. Some portraits. School contracts." He shuddered. "Ugh."

"Didn't like it, huh?"

"I'd rather eat slugs."

Kate laughed. "How did you manage to get into something you hated?"

"Easy. I was an art major in college. Thought I wanted to be a commercial artist. When I graduated I went to work for Adtech. Stuck it out for six years, then I decided I couldn't handle the neon lights any longer."

"Neon lights?"

"Yeah. I worked all day in a seven-by-eight-foot

cubicle on the fourteenth floor. No windows. Just neon lights. And I had to wear a tie."

"A tie? Hey, I'd quit right there."

"You're laughing at me."

"Mmmm."

Dave carefully turned onto A Street. "It just wasn't the way I pictured my life. Every year I felt I'd lost a little more control over my own destiny. Every year I made more money and felt like less of a success. So I quit. Unfortunately, the rent still had to be paid, so I decided to try photography. I'd done a lot of it at Adtech. It seemed okay in theory. I'd be my own boss, make my own hours, pick out my own clothes. In reality, it was boring, and incredibly time-consuming, and frustrating because there was so little creativity involved."

"I guess I'm lucky to have found something I really loved so early in life."

It was a simple statement, but she had said it with such an incongruous mixture of joy and wistfulness that Dave felt his throat close. He stole a glance at her and reached for her hand, taking it in his, giving it a gentle squeeze. A part of him envied her success. She'd found her niche, found something she excelled at and enjoyed. But another part of him wondered about making lifelong choices during childhood. It wouldn't have been for him.

He double-parked the truck in front of Kate's house and watched the men pile out behind them. "You order the pizza, and I'll get the furniture squared away."

Kate gave him a thumbs-up sign. "I'm going to put Elsie in the guest bedroom on the second floor until I get the roof and ceiling fixed."

"Sounds good."

Half an hour later the Potatoes had installed a double bed and small dresser for Elsie, and had removed the debris from Kate's room and set up her new queen-size bed. She stood with a stack of linens in her arms while the men trooped out her door and hopped the porch railing over to Dave's house. "We have to do men's stuff now," Dave told her. "We have to go over to my place and watch a hockey game on the tube and drink beer and bore the hell out of one another."

"If it's so boring, why do you do it?"

"It's traditional. Only married guys get excused from having this much fun." He thought about it a minute. "Want to get married?"

"I'd sooner get boiled in oil. Nothing personal."

"And after everything I've done for you, you won't do this one small favor for me. Okay, so you won't marry me. How about taking me to the concert."

She looked skeptical. "You really want to go to the concert?"

"With all my heart. I can't think of anything I'd rather do than go to your concert."

"I find that hard to believe."

"Actually, it's my second choice," he admitted. "I didn't think you'd go for the first."

Kate rolled her eyes and tried to leave, but he took her arm. "Wait! I swear, I really want to go to the concert." It was the truth. He needed to know more about her. He was besotted! He wasn't even sure he'd been joking when he'd asked her to marry him. "I love cello concerts," he told her earnestly. "How many celli will be playing?"

"It's a chamber music group, and I'm the only cellist."

"That's even better. I love chamber music."

Kate suspected he didn't know chamber music from white bread. She thought he looked like the type to nod off and fall out of his seat five minutes after the lights were dimmed, and she found that prospect devilishly appealing. Sometimes these things could get a little dull. "I'm going to make the beds, take a shower, and then I'll be ready to go. About half an hour. It's at the National Academy of Sciences, and the dress is casual."

An hour later Kate walked onstage in the intimate NAS auditorium. She looked past the footlights and found Dave on the aisle in the sixth row. She was accustomed to people watching her, but not with such unwavering curiosity, not with such indolent sexuality. He looked very handsome in a custom-tailored tweed sport coat, Khaki shirt, and Khaki silk foulard tie. He was sitting behind and slightly to the side of Sydney Mellon, the music critic assigned to the concert. Mellon was a lump of a man. A pear-shaped blob of middle-aged flesh in a camel's-hair blazer and gravy-stained tie. He knew music in and out and would have been a decent critic if it weren't for his habit of falling asleep in the middle of every concert.

Kate acknowledged the audience and sat on the plush padded folding chair. She positioned her cello between her legs and cleared her mind of everything but the job at hand. In some ways she liked these small concerts best. Each nuance of tone, each phrase, was critical. She liked being directly responsible for the mood of her audience. She was a woman who rose to a challenge, who enjoyed the pleasures of a task well done.

If Kate was a born performer, David Dodd was a born observer. He noticed details and added them up like a mathematician doing addition. He wasn't necessarily judgmental, but he formed opinions, changing them when necessary and storing them away for possible future use. He found Kate to be an especially intriguing personality. Not only had she stolen his heart, but she filled his mind as well. And he was enthralled as he watched the artist quietly but firmly take over the woman. Her face became a professional mask of total concentration. Her curly red hair had been swept back with jade combs into an elegant style. Her eyes were enhanced with a smudge of shadow. Her complexion was that of a porcelain doll. She wore a floor-length black taffeta skirt that was nipped at the waist with a simple two-inch band, and rustled when she walked. Her blouse was a high-necked puff-sleeved Victorian in crisp white organdy over a satin camisole. The front of the blouse was plain, leaving nothing to detract from her high, rounded breasts. A column of small pearl buttons marched down the back of the blouse so that it seemed impossibly inaccessible. Dave couldn't imagine how she'd gotten herself into it, and couldn't imagine how he'd ever get her out of it. It was a chastity belt of sorts, he decided. A would-be lover's nightmare.

As the opening duetto ended, and the audience applauded, Dave shifted in his seat. He'd been so absorbed in watching Kate that he hadn't heard a single note.

In front of him, Sydney Mellon's soft pink chin sunk to his chest, his eyes drooped closed, and his lips rhythmically pouted and parted in little puffs of breath. His pad and pencil remained poised on his small paunch, held tight by a hand that had developed a reflex grip much like a bird uses to sleep on a perch.

There were artists who'd been mortally insulted by Mellon's catnaps, but Kate was oblivious. Even if she'd known the critic was sleeping, she wouldn't have cared. She was alive with the beauty of the moment; Gioacchino Rossini's music flowed from her cello in resonant waves of controlled emotion. A slight flush had risen to her cheeks and a curl had worked loose from the jade comb. Dave leaned forward, totally entranced by the music and the woman.

Kate paused, turned the page, and began the final allegro. Mellon's eyes flashed open and his head snapped up with a snort that could be heard fifteen rows back. It was the first time Kate could ever remember being jolted out of place in the middle of a piece. She improvised a few bars and almost dropped her bow when she saw Dave roll up his program and smack Mellon on the top of his shiny bald skull.

Later, when they were in the car, driving home, she turned to Dave and grinned. "That was a nice shot you gave Sydney."

It took a minute for Dave to connect. "Sydney?"

"The somnolent sitting in front of you."

Dave's eyebrows shot up. "Do you believe that guy? He fell asleep. He's lucky I only smacked him on the top of his head."

"That was the music critic for the paper. He always falls asleep. Usually he doesn't wake up until intermission. I must have been a little loud on the allegro."

Dave parked in front of the house and cut the lights. "You were perfect on the allegro. I can't ever remember hearing anything more beautiful." He reached over and removed the combs, running his fingers through her hair to free the curls. "I can't remember ever *seeing* anything so beautiful."

She was used to receiving compliments, but she wasn't used to having them whispered to her in the dark intimacy of a Porsche. The words were as much of a caress as the touch of his hand. They flowed over nerves still strung tight from the concert and sent ripples of excitement coursing along her spine. The excitement burned in her chest and tumbled her stomach. She knew exactly what it was. She'd experienced it many times before. Stage fright, she thought. He was going to kiss her and she was scared to death. It was great. The best part of a performance . . . anticipation. She sat perfectly still, barely breathing, feeling deliciously intoxicated with the moment.

His fingertip traced a feather-light line from her temple to the curve of her chin, and slipped along the nape of her neck. She'd worn a floor-length black velvet cape, and as the velvet felt cool and slick under his hand, the woman beneath was warm and pliant. She shifted toward him, and he thought the sound of her skirt rustling in the dark car was intensely erotic. A passionate woman all wrapped up in a chaste package. Fire and ice. He'd recognized the combination onstage, where she held her audience with her presence as much as her playing.

She curled into the circle of his arms and tilted her face to him. When his lips lowered to hers she gave a low, spontaneous murmur of acquiescence. She felt his hands tighten at the small of her back and felt his mouth move across hers with gentle urgency. If she'd known him longer, she could have admitted to the love that was so obvious in the kiss. And she could have admitted to the love it generated in her. Never before had she felt so desirable or so cherished. She responded with all the honesty and generosity she possessed, returning the kiss, deepening it until she felt as if her blood were boiling in her veins.

Kate heard a faint rapping, and pulled away from David. Outside the car Elsie was shaking her head.

"What are you two doing in there? I can hardly see anything with those windows all steamed up."

Dave leaned over Kate and rolled down the window. "You have a problem, Elsie?"

"Not anymore. I got rid of the guy on the roof. And I took care of the wimp in the backyard too. But with all the slimeballs you've got running loose in this neighborhood, I don't know if I'd want to sit out here, fogging up the windows of this fancy car."

Dave narrowed his eyes. "Guy on the roof? Wimp in the backyard?"

"Listen, I can't stay out here holding a conversation. I'm missing my TV show. I just thought if you two were gonna diddle around out here, you should have this." She lifted a nine-shot, forty-five automatic with a nine-inch barrel to window level and passed it through to Dave.

Kate shrieked and squeezed her eyes shut.

"Holy!" Dave pointed the gun toward the windshield and checked the safety. "What the hell are you doing with this thing?"

"Picked it up at a yard sale. I was gonna use it on the cook at the old people's home but never got around to it."

"You have a license for this gun?"

"Say what?"

Dave hefted the .45. It was of World War II vintage, weighed about five pounds, and he thought it could probably make a hole in a target the size of an orange. Not exactly a lady's gun. "I think we should go in now," he said to Kate. "I'd never get past those buttons on the back of your dress anyway."

Kate opened her eyes. "Shame on you. We're not at the buttons stage."

"I know. I was just thinking about being at the buttons stage."

"Uh-huh."

"It must take you hours to get out of this thing."

"More like seconds. The buttons don't open. They're just for appearance. There's a zipper underneath. Actually, the blouse and the skirt are all one piece. I had it made that way because I'm always late. Clever, huh?"

"Clever doesn't even come close."

Kate acknowledged his appreciation of her easy-to-get-out-of dress with a grim smile. Like Elsie said— the man had plans. The fact that she found those plans appealing was a little frightening. She locked eyes briefly with Dave in a mutual, silent admission of attraction, and then she followed Elsie into the house.

Dave trailed Kate into the kitchen. "So what's this business about someone on the roof?"

Elsie took a seat opposite the portable television on the kitchen table. "It must have been about five-thirty because it was just dark out, and I was putting my stuff away when I heard footsteps up there. They were soft. Someone was being real careful, but I got ears like an elephant. I hear everything. So I went up to the third floor, and sure enough, some-one was sliding that piece of fence back. I said, 'Hold it right there, or I'll blow your damn brains out,' and then I decided I didn't like the way he looked, so I blasted him one."

Kate felt the blood drain from her face. "My Lord, did you kill him?"

"Nah, he jumped back. Besides, I never shoot to kill. It's better if you get them in the privates. Nobody bothers you once you shoot someone in the privates. Word gets out."

Dave crossed his arms loosely over his chest and tried not to smile. "It'd slow me down."

"I looked out the back window, and there was another one, standing in the yard," Elsie said. "Soon as he saw me he took off."

Dave cocked an eyebrow. "You didn't shoot at him?"

"Well, yeah, I did. Dug up a little ground about six inches in front of his shoe. I was aiming for his foot, but I missed. You see, it's one thing to shoot people in the privates when they're breaking into your house, but you gotta be careful about people that're just in your yard. The police don't like it."

Dave's mouth twitched at the corners. "How'd the guy on the roof escape?"

"He hopped from house to house, and I lost sight of him. This sort of thing happen a lot?" Elsie demanded, looking at Kate.

Kate groaned. "I need a cup of tea."

"I think it's got something to do with the helicopter part," Elsie said. "Those two were looking for something."

Kate put a pot of water on to boil. "Why do you say that?"

"I've seen homeless people with more stuff than you. You'd have to be nuts to try to rob this house."

"Maybe they thought I sold all my furniture to buy drugs, and they were after the drugs."

Elsie snorted. "Are you kidding? Look at you. You dress like Mary Poppins. Everyone knows Mary Poppins doesn't do drugs. That chick took sugar to get her through. You ever hear of someone robbing for sugar? Besides, how'd they know there was a hole in the roof? You think druggies use aircraft to figure these things out? No sir, I tell you those guys were after something. You look around real good when that thing landed in your bed? You find anything else?"

Kate exchanged glances with Dave. "We never really looked for anything else."

Dave slung an arm around Kate. "I'd like to see you over at my house for a minute." He turned to Elsie. "Excuse us."

"Take your time. I'm going to watch the end of this TV show and then I'm going to bed early. Tomorrow I have the morning shift at the café."

Dave wrapped the cape around Kate and hurried her next door, wondering what the devil he was going to say to her when he had her alone. He was having an anxiety attack thinking about leaving her tonight. Her house was disaster prone. Airplane parts fell into it. Then there was the business about the man on the roof. That presented very scary possibilities. Elsie could be right about someone looking for more parts. On the other hand, Elsie could have lied about a man on the roof . . . in which case Elsie was dangerously crazy.

No way did he want Kate to stay in that house tonight. Unfortunately, he didn't have a clue how to prevent her. He couldn't just forbid a grown woman from staying in her own house. He could tell her the truth—that he was in love with her and had gone completely looney tunes. That would be his last resort, he decided. He'd already asked her to marry him, and she'd declined. Of course he hadn't been serious about the proposal, not completely serious anyway. Still, saying she preferred to be boiled in oil was a tad insulting. Maybe he could appeal to her good judgment. Maybe he could lock her in the hall closet. He closed the heavy oak door behind them and hit the light switch. "Listen, Kate, about tonight . . ."

"My Lord, did you see that gun? It was big! It was the biggest gun I've ever seen. It was the *only* gun I've ever seen. She's probably got more of them too. She's probably got a whole arsenal in her bedroom. Grenade launchers and submachine guns." She hung her cape on the hall coatrack. "I knew I should have asked for references. I should have required a psychiatric profile, a urine test, fingerprints . . ."

"Maybe you should refund her money tomorrow."

Kate rustled into the kitchen. "I can't refund her money. I *spent* her money . . . on the furniture."

"I'll loan you whatever you need. I have lots of money. I don't know what to do with all my money."

Kate paced in front of the refrigerator. His jacket probably cost five hundred dollars, she mused. He drove a thirty-thousand-dollar car. And this afternoon he disposed of a case of imported lager without blinking an eye. Either he'd robbed a bank, or else he'd grown up in Toad Hall, and the senior Toad had recently died. "Wedding pictures must pay well."

"Weddings pay next to nothing." He gave her a cat-that-caught-the-canary smile. "I won the lottery."

"Uh-huh."

"I did!"

"Nobody wins the lottery. It's all a hoax. It's done with mirrors."

"Honest. I won the lottery. Five million. Of course, after taxes it was a lot less." He took a small framed photograph from the wall and held it out to her. "My commemorative keepsake."

"Son of a gun. You actually won the lottery."

He put the picture on the counter. "I immediately quit the photography business and haven't had a real job since."

"Then what do you do all day?"

"Whatever I want. Mostly nothing, I guess. Except for my drawing. I spend a reasonable amount of time drawing."

Kate wrinkled her nose. For as long as she could remember, there hadn't been enough hours in her day, and she'd always considered anyone who didn't work a slacker. She had a mental image of David

Dodd with a two-day-old beard, drinking beer and reading comic books. Not a pretty picture. *His* business, she reminded herself. She had no right to sit in judgment on his life-style. If he'd turned himself into a shiftless spud, it was no skin off her nose. She found a knife and whacked off a piece of spice cake.

Dave winced and removed the knife from her hand. "There's something about women and weapons that makes me very nervous."

"Chauvinist."

"Not at all. I also get nervous about men and weapons."

Kate's thoughts returned to Elsie. "So what do you think of my roomie? Is she crazy?"

"I don't know. I'm not excited about her packing that cannon. And I don't know if I buy the story about the guy on the roof." He gave Kate a plate for her cake. "I hate to say this, but underneath it all . . . I like Elsie."

Kate took a swipe at the icing with her finger. "I guess I do too. But if I believe Elsie, then what about the helicopter pod?" She forked a piece of cake into her mouth. "I can't believe someone intentionally bombed my house, but her theory about something else falling down . . . that caught my attention. It would make sense that there was a camera on the camera mount."

Dave pulled food from the refrigerator and lined it up on the counter. Lettuce, roast beef, mustard, horse radish, tomatoes, provolone cheese. He took two rolls from a bakery bag and sliced them. "Smitty and I dragged your bed out and cleaned up the room, and there wasn't anything unusual there."

"How about the third floor?"

Dave piled roast beef on the rolls. "We didn't do much to the third floor. We just made sure nothing else was going to crash down on you." He slapped on cheese and tomatoes. "Still, I think we would have noticed if something extra was lying around."

Kate took the sandwich from him. "Boy, this whole thing is pretty creepy, huh?"

"Mmmm. And why do I get the uncomfortable feeling you're enjoying it?"

"It's curious. Sort of exciting."

"It could be dangerous."

She'd had the same thought. She liked to think of herself as a fairly bold person, but she wasn't foolhardy. After weighing the dangers, she made a decision. "That's why I'm sleeping with you tonight. You don't mind, do you?"

He almost dropped his sandwich in his lap. "Sleeping with me?" Oh, wonderful response, Dave. Lord, he was such a cluck!

"I didn't mean *with* you. I meant *here*. In your guest room. On your couch."

"Sure. I knew that was what you meant."

Kate grinned at him.

He grinned back. "You sort of caught me by surprise."

"We could let Elsie think we were sleeping together, then she wouldn't be insulted."

Her suggestion fueled the fantasy he'd started

months before, and he thought about the zipper running the length of her dress and how easy it would be to slide that zipper down. Oddly enough, tonight it evoked old-fashioned family images. A husband lovingly helping his wife to dress while children waited to go on an outing. Or a husband breathlessly easing the dress from his wife's shoulders, letting it fall of its own weight, rustling as it dropped to the floor in a crumpled pool of black and white material. The fantasy was so powerful it almost made him dizzy. He could hear the zipper move along its tracks, see the look of expectation on her face. Feel his heart pounding in his chest. The latter was no figment of his imagination. The prospect of Kate sleeping under his roof had his pulse racing. He knew it was nonsense. Kid stuff to have these romantic notions. She wasn't going to come creeping into his bed in the middle of the night. It was too soon, and they both knew it. Nevertheless, the need was there, humming below the surface, an itch that wouldn't go away. Her hair was tousled, but the dress still looked starched and prim. She was covered from neck to toes, and Dave couldn't for the life of him understand why that seemed so seductive. Under the white organdy there was the barest outline of her bra: an imprint of beige lace against soft ivory breast. He was sure the memory of that vision would have him thrashing sleeplessly in his bed all night. He raised his eyes to hers, and knew he'd broadcast his thoughts as surely as if he'd spoken them out loud. There'd been plenty of times in his life when he'd had to hide his emotions, and then there were those times when he'd fabricated emotions he didn't feel. This wasn't one of them. Even if he'd wanted to, he couldn't have controlled or disguised the feelings he had for Kate. He flashed her a smile that was ten percent embarrassment and ninety percent warning. "Good idea. We wouldn't want Elsie to get insulted."

Kate swallowed, but the sandwich felt stuck in her throat. She wasn't sure of his exact thoughts, but his eyes were so smoldering that her own desire had slammed into place with a thud. He took her breath away. And the smile was alarmingly obvious. "Now that I think about it further, I might be safer in my own house. . . ."

Dave tipped back in his chair, good-natured amusement replacing deeper emotions. "You could be right, but it'll be more fun if you stay here. We can make popcorn and stay up all night telling ghost stories."

Four

A Street houses seemed impossibly narrow from a pedestrian's point of view, but thanks to ten-foot ceilings and the limited number of rooms, the interiors were surprisingly spacious. Dave had chosen the front room with the half-turret alcove for his upstairs bedroom, and converted the remaining second floor room into a sitting room. It was a comfortably masculine room, Kate thought, slouching into the luxurious oxblood-leather couch. She had changed into a pair of borrowed sweats and thick wools socks and, following Dave's lead, had propped her feet on the coffee table. They sat side by side with the popcorn bowl between them, their eyes glued to the TV, their minds finely tuned to each other's breathing pattern. It was a new feeling for Kate. She'd known other men and shared varying degrees of intimacy with them. And none had been so intimate as Anatole. But she'd never experienced this type of pull. It didn't occur to her to label it love at first sight. In her mind love at first sight was something that happened to Cinderella and Fred Astaire. Love at first sight was when two strangers locked eyes across a crowded ballroom, and the whole rest of the world faded away. Singing and dancing were necessary elements to love at first sight. The feeling she had for Dave was more like locking wire carts at the supermarket. Some humor, some annoyance, and an inability to separate the damn things. The truth was, she didn't want to unlock her cart from Dave's just yet. She felt drawn to him. But more important, under the restless energy of sexual attraction was security, comfort, and satisfaction. How she could derive those stable emotions from an unemployed bum, she couldn't begin to guess. From the corner of her eye she watched the rise and fall of his chest, studied the set of his mouth, and happily concluded he was going through similar agonies. He wanted to touch her, just as she wanted to touch him. She was almost sure of it. And she didn't mind acting on assumptions, since he looked as if he was not going to make a move. "Dave?"

"Uh-huh."

"Are you going to kiss me, or what?"

He grinned at her. "I didn't want to be pushy. I was afraid you might go home."

"Not a chance. You're stuck with me. I'm no Chicken Little, but I'm not unnecessarily brave either. I have a very strong sense of survival."

"And you've decided I'm less dangerous than Pistol-Packin' Elsie?"

"Something like that."

Their eyes held and measured. "I'm not sure my male ego can handle that." But he was secretly flattered.

Kate laughed. "Your male ego seems pretty healthy to me." She sank farther into the couch. "Anyway, it's not just Elsie that has me spooked. It's the house. It's always felt empty, even when it was filled with furniture. When Anatole and I lived there, our furniture was all very sterile and very modern—just like our marriage. Anatole liked it that way, but I never felt comfortable. Now that I'm alone the house still feels"—she searched for a word—"stern. There's no whimsy to it. It doesn't feel friendly. Maybe that's why I've never gotten around to furnishing it. It's a terrific house, but not for me. Now that it has a hole in the roof, it feels downright creepy." She looked at Dave's sitting room walls, which were lined with old photographs and bookshelves filled to brimming, and she smiled with lazy contentment. "Your house feels good. Warm and cluttered with life." She leaned her head back and closed her eyes. "Your house feels safe because you've made it a home, a haven. My house is just a tall, narrow building that attracts disaster." She sat straight up with the force of a sudden decision. "I'm going to sell the dumb thing. I don't need all that room. And I can't afford the mortgage payments without Anatole. And I'm definitely not the landlord type."

Dave took the popcorn bowl and set it on the table. "Where will you live if you sell your house?"

She shrugged. "I'll find another house. One that's more suited to me."

He slid his arm across her shoulders and pulled her close. There was strength to her, he thought. Even as a little girl, as a young musician, she'd known focus, discipline, and passion. It had made her resilient and proud and vital. But there'd been a price. She'd never iced a cake, probably never thrown a football, never papered a bathroom. She lived all alone in an empty house that might be more representative of her life than she realized. He rested his cheek against her silky curls and felt emotions warring inside him. Lots of desire. And an equal amount of protective tenderness. Wonderful Dave, do you want to protect her from yourself? He smiled behind her back, feeling foolishly euphoric.

She snuggled into him, her breasts firmly pressed against the wall of his chest, and her hand splayed at the base of his ribs. He couldn't remember a woman ever seeming so right in his arms. He'd been wanting to hold her since he'd first seen her in the awful black coat. He'd always imagined there'd be fireworks. The brittle, bright light of a sparkler. A flash of fire. But he'd been wrong. When he held Kate it was slow heat. Relentless, inexorable heat. The sort of heat that turned a man molten . . . and when he cooled down would never be in exactly the same shape as before. He nuzzled the curls at her temple and kissed her just above her ear. When she turned her face to him he felt the air burning in his lungs. Her lips were parted in expectation, her eyes were trusting, and a pink flush had spread across her cheeks. He wanted to tell her he loved her, but he knew it would sound ridiculous. How could he be so desperately in love with someone after only twenty-four hours? His finger traced a line along her jaw and his hand slid to the nape of her neck while his mouth lowered to hers. He wanted to know her slowly, to let affection and need build bit by bit over the course of time, but their tongues touched and he felt control rush away from him. He'd thought he'd known passion, but nothing in his thirty-one years had prepared him for the fierce desire that gripped him. It was primitive, raw, uncompromising. He held her tight against himself and kissed her with insatiable, almost painful hunger. Lord, if he felt like this now, where would he be in ten minutes? He'd be done, he thought ruefully. He'd set a new land-speed record for making love. He pushed himself away from her and held her at arm's length. "Time out."

"Is it hot in here? Maybe we should open a window."

He looked at her face and saw she was just as rattled as he was. "You think this is infatuation?"

She rose and walked to the window. "I think this is hell!" She threw the window open and stuck her head out for air. "I have to tell you, Anatole never made me feel like this. Anatole was . . . holy cow, look at this."

Dave joined her at the window. Outside, a bright

beam from a flashlight moved through a neighboring yard, sweeping its length and breadth. Then the light was extinguished, a dark figure scaled what was left of the privacy fence, and the light jiggled across the next yard. Dave pulled Kate away from the window and drew the curtains. They looked at each other with raised eyebrows, exchanging sobering thoughts. "Elsie should have shot higher," Dave said finally.

"We should call the police."

"That guy'll be long gone by the time the police get here." He gave her a fast kiss and wheeled away. "Stay here! I'll be right back."

"Dave!" He was gone, down the stairs, out the front door. "Damn." Kate flew down the stairs after him. "Wait here!" Was he kidding? She was halfway down the street before she realized she wasn't wearing shoes. She looked at her stocking feet, whispered an oath, and stopped dead. She saw Dave round the corner. He was going to meet the guy with the flashlight head on when he got to the last yard on the block. And he might need help. She wasn't sure what sort of help she could provide, but she took off at a run, mindless of the cold pavement under her feet. She turned the corner and saw Dave waiting in the shadow of Frank Schneider's ivy-covered seven-foot fence. The house was dark and obviously empty. There was the subdued sound of someone quietly scaling the fence from the other side of the yard and lithely dropping to the ground. Through the slats in the wooden fence, Kate saw the flashlight switched on again.

They heard footsteps pattering down the narrow gravel alley separating the abutting backs of yards and someone rattling the locked back door to Frank Schneider's fence. When the door wouldn't open, a four-letter word carried to Kate and Dave. Their eyes rolled in disbelief. "Elsie," they said in unison. They reached her just in time to see the barrel of the .45 glint malevolently as she blasted the lock off the door and kicked the door in John-Wayne style. A man burst through the door, knocking Elsie into Kate and Dave. Another shot rang out, a car pulled up to the curb, the man with the flashlight jumped into the car and sped away.

Dave held on to the fence for support and stared down at his foot. The tip of his right shoe had been blown off. "I've been shot!"

"It was an accident," Elsie said. "My trigger finger slipped when that creep knocked into me." She looked at his shoe and snorted. "That don't hardly count for nothing. It barely nicked you. Can you move your toe?"

"Yeah."

"Then it can't be too bad." She shook her head. "They don't make men like they used to."

There was a low growl and the Schneiders' pitbull appeared in the doorway of his doghouse.

Kate took a step backward. "Ohmigod, we woke up Daisy."

Dave turned toward the growl. The ground seemed to shake with stampeding pitbull feet, he saw a flash of white teeth, and felt the jaws of death clamp on to the bottom of his jeans. Daisy? This foaming, homicidal hound from hell was named Daisy?

"Hold still!" Elsie ordered. "I'll shoot the privates off the beast."

Dave gritted his teeth. "Elsie, you better be talking about dog privates!"

Daisy planted her feet, gave a yank, and tore the lower half of Dave's pant leg off. The dog viciously shook its prize, gave Dave one last cursory glance, and slunk back to its doghouse with the shredded denim.

Elsie glared at the departing dog. "Man, that is one dumb pitbull. Satisfied with a piece of your pants. Shoot."

Dave closed the door and propped a garbage can against it. "You sound disappointed, Elsie."

She looked at the gun in her hand. "It's all them missed opportunities."

The thought of Kate on the couch flashed through his head. "Yeah, missed opportunities are always depressing."

"Well, I gotta go home and get some sleep. I got burgers to fry in the morning," Elsie said.

Dave looked at Kate's feet and scooped her into his arms. "Next time you chase down desperadoes, remember to wear shoes."

"I was in a hurry."

Dave opened one eye and looked at his bedside clock. Five-thirty and someone was playing music.

Someone was playing it *loud.* "Damn." It was the only word he was capable of forming. He freed himself from a tangle of sheets, lurched out of bed, and kicked at the clothes on the bedroom floor until he located a pair of jeans. It had to be Kate, but why was she creating this racket in the middle of the night? He tugged the jeans over his hips and ran a hand through his hair, making it even more rumpled than it had been. Narrowing his eyes against the bright light in the hall, he thumped down the stairs and padded barefoot to the kitchen, where he found Kate seated on a straight-back chair with her cello between her legs and a cassette player at her feet.

She glanced up and felt her heart flip. Anatole always looked perfect in the morning. His short blond hair was never out of place, his pajamas barely wrinkled, his chin clean-shaven from the night before. Dave looked like a wild animal. His hair was mussed and curling over his forehead in bangs, like a little boy's. But that was where the little boy stopped. Everything else about him was *man.* His sleepy brown eyes seemed a little annoyed. His soft, full mouth slightly belligerent. His five o'clock shadow sent chills down her spine. His shoulders were broad, his stomach flat, his jeans sat low and mean on his hips, suggesting that was all there was—just jeans. She stared at him open-mouthed, her bow poised in midair.

His voice was low and raspy and threatening. "Lord, Kate, what are you doing? It's the middle of the night and you're peeling the paper off the walls with Eugene Ormandy."

She had to swallow before she answered. Get a grip on yourself, she ordered. She'd seen half-naked men before, hadn't she? But nothing like this, she thought. None that growled and meant it. "It's not Eugene Ormandy."

"Why aren't you asleep?"

"I sleep in only on Sundays. Today is Monday, and on Monday I get up at five and practice until seven, then—"

"The hell you do." He punched the Off button on the tape player, snatched the bow, laid it on the kitchen table, and gently pulled the cello from her. Seemed to him there were better things to put between your legs at five-thirty in the morning, but he refrained from saying so, congratulating himself for his restraint. In one swift movement he had her on her feet, then slung her over his shoulder.

"What are you doing?"

"I'm trying to get some sleep." He stomped up the stairs, extinguished the hall light, and dumped her into his bed. Before she could scramble out he was next to her, a heavy leg thrown over hers, his arm wrapped around her chest. " 'Night."

" 'Night? Are you crazy?"

"No. I'm cranky. I've won the lottery, and I don't get up at five in the morning. Not for anyone. Not if I can help it anyway."

"Are you planning on ravishing me?"

"I'm planning on pinning you down so you can't make any more noise until I'm ready to get up."

"Sounds boring. You sure you're not going to ravish me?"

He looked at her from under lowered lids. "Do you want to be ravished?"

"Um, no."

"Then stop wriggling under me."

She looked at him coyly. "My wriggling bother you?"

His hand tightened on her arm. "Your *breathing* bothers me."

Downstairs, the brass door knocker thunked, and Kate propped herself up on one elbow. "You expecting company for breakfast?"

His response was an oath, barely audible and impressively versatile. He rolled out of bed and went to the window. "Looks like a carpenter."

"A carpenter! I need a carpenter. Don't let him get away." Kate was down the stairs and at the door before Dave had even turned around. She unlatched the chain, popped the dead bolt, and threw the door open. "Yes?"

He was five feet eight with the neck of a linebacker and arms like Popeye. He had red hair, a red beard, and a tool belt hung low on his hips. "Howdy. I'm looking for the lady who owns the house next door. You wouldn't happen to know where she is, would you?"

"That's me."

"I'm Mark Beaman. My sister's married to Nancy Berk's brother."

Dave ambled over and held out his hand. "Nancy Berk is Howard's wife."

"Yeah. Howie called me up last night and said the lady here had a problem with her roof and needed it fixed right away. He asked me if I could help you out."

Dave blinked at him. "It's five-thirty in the morning."

"Yeah. I always start work at five-thirty. That way I'm done by three. Construction hours."

Two hours later Mark was repairing the bedroom ceiling and had hired a subcontractor to do the roof. Kate dropped a gray sweatshirt over her damp hair, pulled on a pair of comfortable jeans, and slid her feet into Docksiders. In lieu of a brushing, she ran her fingers through her hair and cracked her knuckles. She was off schedule. It was seven-thirty, and she still hadn't practiced. At least she'd had her shower. She strapped on her watch and ran next door.

Dave answered with a coffee cup in his hand.

" 'Morning. I left my cello here, and—" The aroma of freshly brewed coffee rushed out at her, almost making her knees buckle. She licked her lips and hoped her nostrils weren't flaring. "And, um, I need to practice."

"Don't you ever get tired of practicing?"

Her eyes widened. Get tired of practicing? What a bizarre thought. "Of course not."

He sipped his coffee, studying her over the rim of his cup, and she found herself bristling under his scrutiny. So what if she got tired of practicing sometimes. It was her job. At least she had a job. At least she had goals. She glared at him, getting more furious by the minute, wondering why she felt so provoked. He'd asked her a simple question in a conversational tone, and she was ready to punch him in the nose. Coffee fumes, she decided, they were making her crazy. Once she had a cup of coffee she'd feel much better. She didn't mind that he'd slung a red flannel shirt on his shoulders, but he still hadn't shaved or combed his hair. She didn't mind that he spent the entire morning reading the *Post* funnies while she barely had time to glance at the front page.

He put his hand to the small of her back and propelled her toward the kitchen. "You have breakfast yet?"

"Of course I've had breakfast. It's seven-thirty, for crying out loud."

"What did you have?"

Kate looked at him blank-faced. Caught like a rat in a trap, she thought. She made a pretense of fussing with her bow and mumbled.

"What?"

She sighed and rolled her eyes. "I said I had a cookie."

"That's it?"

"It was oatmeal. Oatmeal is good for you. Everybody eats oatmeal in the morning." It had been oatmeal with double stuff icing and chocolate chips. But there was no need to go into unnecessary details.

"That's a terrible breakfast. You need juice and milk and a good whole grain cereal. You'll never grow up to be big and strong on cookies for breakfast."

"Thanks, Mom."

He sliced an orange and fed it to the juicer. "I used to be just like you. Always hustling. Always busy." He handed her a glass of freshly squeezed juice. "It's no good for you, you know. Lowers your immune system. You take vitamin C?"

Kate ignored the question and opened a cupboard, searching for a coffee mug. "I don't have much time . . ."

Dave closed the cupboard and placed a mug in her hand. "Here's your mug, but you get coffee only if you promise to sit down and eat breakfast."

"Will breakfast take long?"

"You ever consider yoga? Relaxation exercises?"

"You ever consider a broken nose because you deprived a redhead of her morning coffee?"

He poured her coffee and pointed to a chair. "Sit!"

"Just for a minute."

"Seven minutes. Five minutes for me to make the oatmeal and two minutes for you to eat it."

"Honest-to-God oatmeal? That congealed gluey stuff with lumps in it? Don't you have any *real* cereal? Don't you have Frosted Flakes or Sugar Crisp or Froot Loops?"

Dave slid the bowl of oats into the microwave. "Better watch your step, or I'll make you eat an egg."

"You're too good to me."

"I know. You're lucky to be living next door to a guy like me. I'm a real catch. I'm rich, I make breakfast, and I'm cute."

"Is this a proposal?"

He slapped a place mat in front of her. "Nope. Last time I proposed you said you'd rather be boiled in oil. Now it's your turn to do the proposing."

"I'd sooner be boiled in oil."

Mark Beaman's footsteps creaked overhead as he tore out the splintered boards and hammered others into place. Country and western music blared from a boom box somewhere on the second floor while a power saw whined outside the kitchen window. Kate tapped her foot and pressed her lips together. It was noon and she still hadn't been able to practice. Carpenters and roofers asked her lots of questions. They required cold sodas, deli hot dogs, bathroom privileges, and unrestricted use of the phone to order supplies they had thought they didn't need. Concentrate, she ordered herself. She was a professional. She should be able to work under trying circumstances, right? Right. She narrowed her eyes and began again.

Mark rumbled into the kitchen. "Howdy."

Kate gritted her teeth and lowered the bow. "Howdy."

"Just passing through. Don't let me disturb you." He went out the back door.

Kate took a deep breath and adjusted her music. Mark reappeared with a sheet of plywood, edged past her, and smiled pleasantly. "You don't play much, do you? I've been waitin' to hear something come out of that thing, but it seems mostly you just sit there, gritting your teeth. You shouldn't do that, you know. It's bad for your head muscles. You're gonna end up with a migraine."

Kate thunked her head down on her music stand. This wasn't going to work. She moved to the living room and set up in front of a window. Roy Orbison still wailed down at her, but at least she wasn't in the traffic pattern. It was pleasant in the front room. The old-fashioned windows stretched almost from the floor to the ceiling, throwing the bright midday light over the glossy, dark wood floor. Across the street Emily Pearson was polishing her brass door knocker. A cluster of Indian corn tied with a pumpkin-colored bow had been hung to the side of the knocker, and a pot of orange mums sat in a redwood container on the front stoop. Despite her resolve to concentrate, Kate found herself staring at Emily Pearson. This was the reason she practiced in the kitchen, she thought. There were too many distractions in the front room. It was almost impossible not to spy on the outside world through the big windows.

In another neighborhood there might have been pictures of pilgrims or Thanksgiving turkeys drawn by children in the downstairs windows, but A Street boasted only adult decorations. The houses were too small for families with teenagers and too expensive for families just starting out. A Street was devoid of backyard swings and the clatter of Big Wheels racing over its brick sidewalks. It was something Kate had never noticed . . . until now. It seemed like a simple observation, but it hit Kate in the pit of her stomach. And she wasn't sure why. She leaned forward in her chair, nose almost pressed against the glass, and wondered where all the children were. Had they all been exported to the suburbs? To the large yards of northern Virginia? Were they living in the bigger houses of northwest Washington?

Emily Pearson saw Kate at the window and waved. She was Kate's age, maybe a little older. A lawyer. Kate waved back and wondered if Emily wanted kids. Emily, with the appropriate door decorations and matching planters and clean windows. Emily would make a great mother. And she'd make a lousy mother, Kate thought. She'd probably misplace her kids on the way to rehearsal and get arrested for abandonment.

As Kate stared outside, Elsie walked past the window. She marched up the front stairs, let herself in, hung her coat on the rack in the foyer, and dropped a white paper bag into Kate's lap. "I'm off my shift, and I brought you a burger.

Kate unpeeled the wrapper. "Everyone's trying to feed me today."

"That's 'cause you're so skinny. Everybody takes pity on you."

Kate smiled. She was getting used to Elsie: rough on the outside, soft on the inside. "This looks good," Kate said. Lettuce, tomato, paper-thin onion, slices of dill pickle, melted cheese, mustard, ketchup, grilled sesame seed bun, and an inch-and-a-half thick barbecued hamburger. She chomped into it and closed her eyes. "Yum."

Elsie folded her arms across her chest and looked down at Kate. "We need to talk."

A glob of catsup emerged from the back end of the hamburger and slopped over Kate's fingers. It mixed with pickle juice and dribbled onto the paper bag spread across her lap.

Elsie made a disapproving sound and pressed on. "Not that it's any of my business, but do you always sleep next door?"

"Not always."

"Well, there's things you should know about him. He comes into the café all the time, all hours of the day, and he never wears a suit. I got it figured out though. I think he's a spy."

"Why do you think he's a spy?"

"It all adds up. You see an ounce of fat on that man? No sir, that boy's in fine shape. He's got a spy butt if I ever saw one. Child, that butt works out. It's ready for action. And another thing, where do you suppose he gets all his money? Flashy car, expensive house."

"Do spies make a lot of money?"

"James Bond isn't hurting."

Kate chewed her hamburger. "True."

"Explains your helicopter part too. I knew from the beginning that was no accident. Some sucker dropped that thing on the wrong house. They were aiming for Dave's house. That David person is a marked man. This here's Washington. This here's Spy Central."

"Sorry to disappoint you, but he's not a spy. He was a down and out photographer, and he won the lottery."

"Get out. No one wins the lottery."

"He did. I saw a picture of the ticket and of him getting his money." She crumpled the hamburger wrapper into the bag. "That was a great hamburger. Thanks."

Mark Beaman sauntered down the stairs and saluted the women on his way to the kitchen. "Howdy."

"Carpenter," Kate explained to Elsie. "He's fixing the ceiling."

"Don't look too bright."

"He's okay."

Elsie snorted. "Don't know much about music."

"He's from Virginia."

"That'll do it." Elsie turned toward the stairs. "It's time for my afternoon nap. I get real grouchy if I don't get my nap. And I'm never gonna be able to sleep with that pathetic whining going on. You don't suppose Mr. Muscle'd mind if I throw his radio out the window, do you?"

"Gee, why didn't I think of that."

Five

Kate squinted at her watch in the darkness. Six o'clock. She was late, and Washington was gridlocked. So what was new? She cracked her knuckles and drummed her fingers on the steering wheel. Less than a mile from her house. So near and yet so far, she thought grimly. She looked at her watch again. One minute past six. If traffic wasn't moving by 6:15, she was going to leave the car in the middle of the road and walk home. The hell with it. Let them tow it away. She inched forward and stopped. One block more and she'd turn onto First Street. "Come on, First Street!" she urged. Wonderful. Talking to yourself while stuck in traffic was a sign of mental instability. She sunk lower in her seat and tried to relax. This was her own fault, she thought. She had taken on too many private students, and now she couldn't fit them all in. Every Monday she was stuck in this mess because her lessons ran late. Someone was going to have to go. But that was easier said than done. She liked all her students. And she needed the money; now that Anatole was gone, the house payments were killing her. Tomorrow she'd try to find time to call a realtor.

At six-thirty she backed into a parking place in front of her house and hurtled out of the car. She grabbed a grocery bag, crooked her finger around a nylon tote bag filled with sheet music, slung her big black purse over her shoulder, and slammed the car door shut with her foot. She turned and bolted for the stairs, barely stifling a scream, when Dave rose from the shadows of her small front porch. "Damn." She leaned against the wrought iron railing and took a deep breath.

"Sorry, I didn't mean to scare you."

"It's not your fault. I wasn't paying attention, and you took me by surprise." She sighed and straightened. "You do that a lot."

He took the grocery bag and the key and opened her front door. "The carpenters and roofers left at three. They'll be back tomorrow to finish up. Elsie went to a bingo game at her church. Your mother called and wanted to know what I was doing in your house. . . ."

Kate rolled her eyes.

"I explained I was keeping an eye on the carpenter, but I don't think she believed me, so I invited her to dinner on Saturday."

"Oh, no! How could you have done such a thing? My mother will expect real food. She'll want to sit at a table and eat off real dishes. Last time my mother came to my house for dinner she left with a migraine that lasted for three days." Kate switched on the lights and looked at her empty living room. "My mother will be wearing heels and stockings. She'll expect to sit in a chair. I haven't got a chair," she wailed. "And worst of all, she'll bring my father."

Dave set the bag on the kitchen counter and began unpacking. Graham crackers, cream cheese, a bag of carrots, quart of skim milk, and strawberry yogurt. "Boy, you really get uptight about your parents."

Kate took the yogurt and dug for a spoon in her silverware drawer. "My parents are very traditional people. They live in a house with furniture."

Dave grinned. "Not to worry. I didn't invite them to your house for dinner. I invited them to *my* house. I figured they'd want to check me out."

"Ohmigod."

He liked shaking her composure every once in a while. It made her more accessible, less driven. Her music was wonderful and special, but Kate needed a little diversity. He watched her return to the yogurt and wondered if that was her supper. "I have some steaks next door. I could put them on the grill."

"Can't. I work with a youth orchestra on Monday nights. Sectional couch." She washed the yogurt down with a glass of spring water and grabbed a banana. "I'm supposed to be there at seven." She looked at her watch and groaned.

"Is it very far?"

"No. I'll make it." She shoved a packet of music into her purse and pulled a hooded sweatshirt over her head. "I have to buy a coat. Maybe Saturday." She hadn't directed the last two sentences to Dave. She'd been thinking aloud. Talking to herself again. Her mind was already jumping ahead to the evening's rehearsal. They'd be playing Beethoven's Pastorale. Working on the last two movements . . . Suddenly she was whirled around and pulled against the wall of Dave's chest with enough force to take her breath away. Their eyes locked for the briefest of moments, long enough to make her heart race. Long enough for her to see the anger, the determination, the frustration. She expected words, but instead she got a kiss. A kiss that was almost violent in its intensity.

He released her, wondered how his heart was standing the strain, and bent to retrieve the purse she'd dropped on the floor.

Kate reluctantly opened her eyes; her lips felt exquisitely swollen. "Of course, I could always stay home. . . ."

Dave hung the black bag on her shoulder and opened the front door. "Wouldn't want to keep you from your obligations. Just making sure you'd remember me."

At two A.M. Dave was awakened by the deep *thwup, thwup, thwup* of a helicopter flying low over the neighborhood. When it buzzed his house for the third time, he slid out of bed, crept across the dark room, and silently stood at his window, watching the blinking lights move across the sky. The helicopter returned to A Street, hovered for a full minute while it beamed light down on rooftops and yards, and then peeled away. The *thwup, thwup thwup* faded in the distance, but Dave remained at the window.

Kate had heard it too. At least the roof was fixed, she'd thought. It still needed to be tarred, but it was patched over and she didn't feel quite so vulnerable. Not that she expected someone to drop through the roof James-Bond style, but after the past two days, anything was possible. She'd gone to the window, just as Dave had, and when the noise was no more than a faraway hum, Kate took stock of her neighborhood by moonlight. It was very dark, very still, very somber. A lifeless cityscape of drawn shades and brick facades. Trees were nude of leaves. Grass was sparse. The occasional splash of colorful mums was muted in shadow. Her postage-stamp front yard was mostly ivy. She'd always wanted to plant flowers, but time had a way of escaping her. At least there was a flowering dogwood. And there was the azalea, but now that she and Elsie had squashed it, she wasn't sure if it would survive the winter. Poor dead azalea, she thought, looking down at it from her second floor window. A piece of plastic lodged deep in the middle of the bush reflected moonlight back to her. She stared at it dully before turning from the window and padding back to bed. She punched her pillow into shape, pulled the quilt over herself, and froze. "Son of a gun."

Dave thought he was seeing things. Kate looked like an apparition, gliding ghostly white down the porch steps in her long flannel nightgown. She was barefoot, moving quickly over the little boxwood hedge that lined her front walk, into the black ivy. She stooped over the azalea, picked up something, straightened, and looked directly up at him, as if she'd sensed his eyes on her. And she had a video camera in her hand!

Five minutes later she sat wrapped in a wool blanket on Dave's couch sipping hot cocoa, waiting for Dave to rewind the tape that had been lodged in the mangled camera.

He draped an arm around Kate and pressed the play button on the remote. A number appeared on the TV screen. Six digits. There were several seconds of blank tape and then an aerial view of A Street materialized. The field of vision narrowed as the image was focused. The lens swept across Kate's backyard, her roof, the empty road, and ran across a house on the opposite side of the street. The exact same route was repeated three times.

On the fourth pass a voice broke in above the chopper noise. "Get the blue sedan."

The picture danced with vibration but held fast to the car as a man emerged, glanced up at the helicopter, and returned to the car. The vibration grew worse, and the picture lost clarity. There was the voice again. "One of the mounts is loose. See if you can—" The screen filled with blue sky and then abrupt blackness.

Dave hit the remote button to rewind the cassette. "He was right. The mount was loose."

"Do you have any idea what this was all about?"

"No. But I know where to get the answer." He reached for the cordless phone on the coffee table and dialed. "Howard? This is Dave. I have your tape."

Kate's eyes got wide. "Howard Berk? How do you know?"

"I recognized his voice. At least I think I recognized his voice." He returned the phone to the table. "That was his answering machine. Now all we have to do is wait for him to wake up."

"This is very creepy. Why would Howard Berk be making videos of my house?"

"My guess is your house was incidental. It happened to be in the flight path. You know anything about the people living in the other house on the tape?"

Kate pushed out her lower lip while she thought about it. "Not much. That's a rental property. They moved in about the same time you did. Don't you know them?"

"No. Lots of different people go in and out. No one ever says hello."

"Maybe they're spies."

"More likely they're musicians who've forgotten to pay their parking citations." He ran a fingertip along the line of her chin. "Are you tired?"

"Out on my feet." She'd had a full day, and the cocoa was warm in her stomach. She felt her eyelids droop and blinked them open.

Dave sighed and scooped her into his arms. He carried her into his room and tumbled her into bed. "Are you *too* tired?"

Kate laughed. "If I say yes, do I get kicked out of this bed?"

"If you say yes, you get to sleep here alone tonight."

He'd smiled when he'd said it, but she knew he was serious. All she had to do was hold out her hand and he'd be next to her. It was enormously tempting. She couldn't think of anything nicer than to spend the night wrapped in his arms. She'd known Anatole for a hundred years, slept with him for two, been married to him for one year, and she'd never felt this close, this comfortable, this loving toward him. David Dodd inspired trust. He was fun. He was intelligent. He was sensitive and sexy. Make that *very* sexy. She was about to invite him to share the bed when she inadvertently yawned.

Dave grimaced. "Guess that answers my question." He tucked the quilt around her and bent to kiss her good-night. His lips brushed over hers, settling gently, their mouths parted, and the kiss deepened.

Kate wound her arms around him and pulled him closer. "You shouldn't jump to conclusions."

His response was swift and silent, his hands taking possession a heartbeat ahead of his mouth. He planned to marry this woman, and if he did, he'd remain married to her for the rest of his life. Put in that perspective, this night should seem insignificant. He should be able to lay this night aside and wait for another evening. A more romantic evening with all the traditional trappings. But he knew that was nonsense. He'd lost all perspective. Kate brought out a response in him that ripped through logic and challenged his self-control. His hands roamed under the nightgown with deliberate exploration. Massaging, teasing, arousing.

Flesh met where clothes had been discarded, and they were lost to their passion. Nothing was forbidden. Everything was sacred. Whatever pleasure they'd anticipated had been pale compared to the reality. They devoured each other. First with their eyes, then with their mouths. There was little rational thought. They were guided by instinct and desperation, moving to assuage the ache of desire, sliding to the edge together. He dove deeper and deeper into her, loosing himself, and taking her with him into the abyss.

Afterward there weren't any words that could adequately explain what had just taken place, so they didn't speak. They remained entwined, ignoring the tangled sheet and scattered bedclothes, neither wanting to feel alone even for a second.

It was barely light when Kate awoke. She took a moment to orient herself, to come to terms with the warm form beside her. Someone was hammering in the distance. The carpenter, she thought. No, that was yesterday. She heard Dave swear and roll away from her.

He pulled on his jeans before he walked to the window and pulled the curtain aside. "Howard Berk, of course." He glanced at Kate. "Maybe you'd better get dressed."

Kate pushed the hair from her eyes. "I haven't any clothes. I came over here in my nightgown."

He shrugged into a shirt and grinned. "What's mine is yours."

She squirmed out of bed. "Nicely put."

His smile broadened. He gave her a loving pat on her bare bottom, took the tape from the dresser top, and prepared to saunter down the stairs. "Guess I'll go let old Howie in."

By the time the door was opened, Howard Berk's knuckles were bruised. He grinned affably at Dave and shoved his hands into his pants pockets. "Got your message."

Dave motioned him in. "Coffee?"

"I'd kill for a cup of coffee."

"Bad choice of words, Howie."

"Figure of speech."

"Uh-huh." Dave padded barefoot to the kitchen and plugged in the coffee maker. "So what's going on?"

Howard slouched in a kitchen chair. "Not much." He pointed to the cassette Dave had placed on the counter. "That the tape?"

"Yup."

"Looks like it's in okay shape."

"Yup."

Howard sighed. "How did you know to call me?"

"You recorded your voice while you were taping, and I recognized it when we played it back." He sliced three pumpernickel bagels and slid them under the broiler. "Jeez, Howard, don't they teach you anything in spy school? Don't you watch television?"

Howard laughed. "I'm not a spy. I'm an undercover cop. I'm telling you since you've already seen the tape; we've had that house across the street under surveillance for the past three months. I even joined the Potatoes as an excuse to be in the neighborhood."

Dave added water and ground Columbian to the coffee maker. He put the toasted bagels on a plate and set them on the table with a tub of cream cheese. "You think they're practicing a little chemistry in their basement?"

"I'm not at liberty to say, but, if I were you, I wouldn't light a match on that side of the street."

"Gotcha." He poured Howard a cup of coffee and sat opposite him. "The quality of the tape isn't all that good. Lots of vibration. You're going to have to isolate a frame and use some high resolution."

Howard studied him as he chewed his bagel. "Do we have a face?"

"Yup. Looked right up at you."

He nodded. "It was worth it, then."

Kate joined them. "It was worth a hole in my roof?"

Howard looked apologetic. "It was an accident."

"Some accident. You could have killed me. And what about trying to break into my house?"

"We weren't trying to break into your house. We were searching the roof. The house was supposed to be empty. I pulled the fence section back to see if there was any evidence of the recorder crashing through the hole, and some crazy old lady almost blew my brains out!"

Dave spread cream cheese on a bagel and refrained from commenting on the location of Howard's brains. He looked up at Kate and caught her smiling and knew she'd had the same thought.

"Then she took a shot at my partner. She have a license for that bazooka?"

Dave refilled Howard's cup. "Absolutely. You want another bagel?"

"Better not. My wife has me on a diet."

"So last night you tried a look-around in the helicopter?"

"Yeah. We were in the neighborhood, doing support for a car chase and thought we'd give it one last shot. Sometimes things show up with the spot that don't show up in daylight. But we didn't find anything. Where was it?"

"In my azalea," Kate said. "I saw it from my second story window."

Howard pushed back from the table and picked up the cassette. "I'm surprised it wasn't ruined by the rain. Do you still have the camera?"

Dave handed him a box filled with the camera pieces. "Playing basketball on Thursday?"

"Yeah. You?"

"Probably."

Howard tucked the box under his arm and looked longingly at the remaining bagel. "I've got to go. I'm late for a briefing."

Dave grinned. "Be a shame to waste that bagel, Howard."

"You know what she gave me for breakfast? Half a grapefruit and a slice of whole wheat bread. And then she gave me my choice of margarine or jelly. She said it was too many calories if I had both."

Dave clucked his tongue. "Cops need more than that. Suppose you got shot today because you were weak from food deprivation?"

Howard's face was a study in solemnity. "You're right, Dodd. I could very well die for lack of that margarine." He spread a thick layer of cream cheese on the bagel. "As much as I hate to do this, I'm going to have to eat this whole bagel."

Dave saw him to the door. "Do me a favor, Howie, next time bag the helicopter and shoot from my window."

When Dave returned to the kitchen Kate had finished her coffee and was rinsing out her cup. He shook his head. "Oh-oh, I don't like the looks of this."

"I'm late!"

"How could you be late at seven-thirty in the morning?"

"I go to an exercise class at eight and a rehearsal at ten. Then at one o'clock I'm giving a noonday recital in a nursing home in Arlington. I have students from three to five. That means I'll get stuck in rush hour traffic again. But I don't have to be at the Kennedy Center until eight tonight. . . ."

"I thought maybe I could take you someplace nice for dinner."

"I'm sorry, I don't have time for dinner." Her regret was genuine. She would have liked to spend an hour or two holding hands and talking. Something important had happened the previous night, and she didn't want to treat it casually.

"Will I see you after the performance tonight?"

"Yes! That'd be great." She ran upstairs and retrieved her nightgown. "I have to go to a reception immediately following, but I should be home around twelve."

He caught her by the waist and drew her to him. His kiss was gentle and lingering. "Be careful driving. You rush around too much."

"My day is too short. I need two more hours."

He'd already reached the same conclusion. She had no Dave time.

Six

Kate sprinted from the car to her front porch and swore profusely when her house key balked in the lock. She jiggled the key, counted to ten, and closed her eyes in relief when the door swung open. There'd been a minor accident on Constitution Avenue that had backed traffic up clear to Virginia. The house was dark and silent. Obviously Elsie wasn't home. She checked her watch. Seven-ten. That was worthy of a few more four-letter words. Kate flung her purse and her packages on the floor and ran up the stairs. It took her thirty seconds of trying various light switches before she realized she had no electricity. She looked out her bedroom window and saw light in other houses on A Street. It had to be her circuit breaker. She snatched a flashlight from her dresser drawer and took off for her cellar. She had her hand on the cellar doorknob when she saw the yellow note tacked at eye level. "Kate, Beaman accidentally cut through a power line. Electrician will be around in morning. Dave." She grabbed a dinner plate drying in the dish drain and smashed it on the floor. "Feel better?" she asked herself. No. She'd have to smash service for eight to feel better today. Now what? She needed a fast shower, and she couldn't take it in the dark. She returned to her bedroom, threw lingerie, shoes, and makeup in her bag, and took her black cape and a black velvet gown from her closet.

She knocked at Dave's door, but no one answered, so she let herself in and found him on the kitchen floor, playing with a train. He'd set up an elaborate system of tracks with tunnels and fake mountains and railroad crossings that flashed red lights.

He looked up when her shoes entered his field of vision. "Do you believe this? Isn't this great? Listen to this, I can make it sound just like a steam engine. . . ."

Kate looked at him coolly. He was thirty-one years old, and he was on his hands and knees playing with a choo-choo. And that wasn't the worst of it. She was falling in love with him. Katherine Finn was falling in love with a man who spent his entire day playing with choo-choo trains. While she was scrambling from one activity to the next, trying to earn a living, trying to become a better cellist, trying to be a good teacher, David Dodd was perfecting the sound of steam. It was frightening. She didn't have the time or the emotional energy to come to terms with it now, so she filed it away. "Would it be all right if I use your shower?"

"Sure. Do I get to scrub your back?"

"No."

"How about your front? I can do amazing things with soap."

"No! I'm in a hurry."

He followed her upstairs. "You're always in a hurry. You need to slow down. . . ."

"I don't want to slow down. I like being busy."

Dave took the gown from her and hung it in his closet. She was crackling with energy. Her green eyes flashed at him, and her hair looked as if it might catch fire at any minute. No wonder they called her the Formidable Finn, he thought. Although he knew he should keep quiet, he couldn't resist making one further comment. "Don't you think your day seems just a smidgeon crowded?"

She kicked her shoes off and pulled the sweater over her head, leaving her in jeans and a long-sleeved white shirt. "I'll admit I could benefit from a little organization, but I love all the things I do. Even the practicing. You know, I can't wait to get up in the morning and sit down with my cello. That's why I practice so early. It isn't to get it over with, it's because I can't wait any longer to play, to perfect a new piece, to enjoy an old favorite." He couldn't understand that, she thought, because he had no purpose to his life. He was a couch potato. He'd reverted back to childhood. He was a wasteoid. He was the man of her dreams, and she was afraid living with him would be a nightmare. His laziness and lack of motivation would drive her crazy. And what would happen when he frittered away his five million? Sad, she thought. Very sad. She sighed at him and shook her head. "Poor Dave."

He didn't know what that meant, but he didn't think it sounded good. "Poor Dave?"

"Your life is boring!"

"How can you say that? I bought a train today."

Kate pressed her lips together, feeling her anger rise. He wasn't perfect. Dammit. He'd made her care about him, and now he was turning out to have a major character flaw. She'd been daydreaming about him all day. She'd considered a relationship. She'd even thought about marriage. And here he was, playing with trains. "You know what you're doing?" she said. "You're raining on my parade."

"Want to run that by me again?"

"When are you going to grow up?"

"I am grown-up."

She stormed off to the bathroom. "You're not grown-up. You spend your whole day playing."

He raised his eyebrows. "So do you. You play your cello."

"Well, of course I play my cello. That's a different kind of play. That's a figure of speech," she sputtered. She locked herself in the bathroom, stripped, and jumped into the shower. Good thing she was

OPEN YOUR HEART TO LOVE.
YOU'LL BE LOVESWEPT WITH THIS FREE OFFER

HERE'S WHAT YOU GET:

1. **FREE!** SIX NEW LOVESWEPT NOVELS! You get 6 beautiful stories filled with passion, romance, laughter, and tears...exciting romances to stir the excitement of falling in love... again and again.

2. **FREE! A BEAUTIFUL MAKEUP CASE WITH A MIRROR THAT LIGHTS UP!** What could be more useful than a makeup case with a mirror that lights up*? Once you open the tortoise-shell finish case, you have a choice of brushes...for your lips, your eyes, and your blushing cheeks.

*(batteries not included)

3. SAVE! MONEY-SAVING HOME DELIVERY! Join the Loveswept at-home reader service and we'll send you 6 new novels each month. You always get 15 days to preview them before you decide. Each book is yours for only $2.09 — a savings of 41¢ per book.

4. **BEAT THE CROWDS!** You'll always receive your Loveswept books before they are available in bookstores. You'll be the first to thrill to these exciting new stories.

BE LOVESWEPT TODAY — JUST COMPLETE, DETACH AND MAIL YOUR FREE-OFFER CARD.

FREE – LIGHTED MAKEUP CASE!
FREE – 6 LOVESWEPT NOVELS!

- NO OBLIGATION
- NO PURCHASE NECESSARY

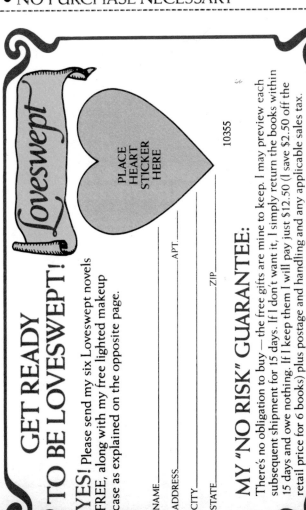

REMEMBER!

- The free books and gift are mine to keep!
- There is no obligation!
- I may preview each shipment for 15 days!
- I can cancel anytime!

(DETACH AND MAIL CARD TODAY.)

BUSINESS REPLY MAIL

FIRST-CLASS MAIL   PERMIT NO. 2456   HICKSVILLE, NY.

POSTAGE WILL BE PAID BY ADDRESSEE

Loveswept

Bantam Books
P.O. Box 985
Hicksville, NY 11802-9827

NO POSTAGE
NECESSARY
IF MAILED
IN THE
UNITED STATES

late, she thought. If she'd had more time, she'd have burst into tears.

Dave knew she would break their date, but he waited anyway, listening for the sound of her car. She came home a little before twelve and went to her house, not his. He wanted to believe she'd merely gone home to change, but in his heart he knew better. She was angry with him because she thought he lacked ambition. She thought fun was frivolous. She didn't like trains. He cringed at the thought of her discovering his attic. His most prized possessions were in the attic, and she'd *hate* them. She'd think he was a total fruitcake. Upstairs he had: two hundred and twelve issues of *Spider-Man* comic books; his Spike Jones record collection; his Dick Tracy decoder ring; seventy-three Matchbox cars; a Tonka dump truck and fire engine. And that was just the beginning. He had bubble-gum machines and a pinball machine and a Teddy Ruxpin. "Business investments," he said to his empty house. "Mood music. After all, creative inspiration doesn't come easy. Some people turn to alcohol, some to drugs . . . I like toys."

She avoided him like the plague all day Wednesday, barely waving as she rushed in and out of her house. He was a nice person, but he simply wasn't for her, she told herself. Yessir, nip this romance in the bud, she decided, before it gets impossibly painful. She'd lived with a man who wasn't precisely right, and she knew what happened. Loneliness, frustration, and anger. It was a dead-end street.

"What happened to David Dodd?" Elsie asked while she rooted in the refrigerator, looking for supper. "Haven't seen him around today."

Kate poked in her cup of yogurt and wished it were a hot fudge sundae. "He probably had some pressing business to attend to. Maybe the supermarket got in a new shipment of comic books."

"You sound like someone's standing on your toes. He dump on you?"

Kate wrinkled her nose. "No, he didn't dump on me. There was nothing to dump. It was all in the preliminary stages."

Elsie looked disgusted. "The man has five million dollars and the most tempting butt I've seen in my whole sixty-six years, and you let him get away?"

"Money isn't everything."

"Okay, so what about his butt?"

Kate had to admit, his butt was pretty terrific. She heard herself sigh and gave herself a mental shake. *Pull yourself together Kate.* Go practice some Haydn. That was always a sobering experience.

Elsie took a TV dinner from the freezer and slid it into the microwave. "You know what you need? You need a change of pace. You need to do something different. Take your mind off your problems."

"I don't have any problems."

"Oh, yeah? What was that sigh all about?" She

squinted at Kate. "You're mooning over that Dodd guy."

"I'm not!"

"Then you're stupid. Anyone with an ounce of sense would moon over him."

"Well, maybe I'm mooning a little."

Elsie took her meal out of the microwave and sat at the table. She ate a forkful of macaroni and cheese and sliced a piece of ham. "I don't usually make offers like this, but I can see you need some perking up." She chewed her ham and prodded her green beans trying to decide if they were edible. "Besides, I need a ride," she added. "So how about if I let you go to a bingo game with me tonight."

"Uh—"

"This is your night off, isn't it?"

"Well, yeah—"

"Okay, then it's settled." She finished her dinner and pushed the tray aside. "We better get a move on. I like to get there early so I get a good seat."

Bingo? The Formidable Finn playing bingo? For an entire evening? She rushed after Elsie. "Listen, I'd really like to do this, but I have to—"

Elsie stopped with her coat halfway around her shoulders. "You have to what?"

Kate couldn't think of anything she had to do. She looked at Elsie blank-faced and opened her mouth, but no words came out.

"What? *what* do you have to do?" Elsie asked.

"I . . . have to buy a coat. I don't have a coat to wear."

"So wear your sweatshirt. This isn't no fancy dress ball we're going to. This is a bingo game, for crying out loud."

Kate meekly pulled the sweatshirt over her head. "I don't know if this is such a good idea. I've never been to a bingo game. I wouldn't want to slow you down."

"Don't worry about it. I'll get you all fixed up."

They ran into Dave on the sidewalk in front of Kate's house.

Kate looked from Elsie to Dave. "Is this a setup?"

Dave widened his eyes in exaggerated curiosity. "Going someplace?"

"We're going to a bingo game," Elsie told him. "You can come if you want."

Kate rammed her fists into her hips. "I'm not going if he's going."

"Her nose is outta joint," Elsie told Dave. "What'd you do to her last night?"

"Nothing."

"Well, no wonder," Elsie said. "When I was her age I got grouchy when nobody did nothing to me too." She looked at Kate's little compact with the bashed-in rear bumper and dented side fender, and she looked at Dave's Porsche. "I never arrived at a bingo game in a Porsche before."

"Then we'll take my car," Dave said. "I know how you feel about missed opportunities."

"I thrive on missed opportunities," Kate told them. "In fact, I'm going to miss this one."

Dave wrapped an arm around her and pushed her

forward. "You're going to pass up a bingo game? Hard to believe. You'd better think it over."

"I've thought it over!"

Dave opened the car door and pushed Kate in. "Think about it some more."

Elsie slid in next to Kate and shoved her toward the driver's side. "This car's really something, isn't it? Real leather. Smooth," she said, running her hand over the dash.

Kate moved onto the console, straddling the gearshift. "This car has only two seats. We don't fit in this car."

"Sure we do," Dave said. "It's nice and cozy." He strapped on his seat belt, turned the ignition, and shifted into first, his hand snaking up the inside of Kate's left thigh. "Good thing we're such good friends," he whispered. "I'd hate to have to shift up a stranger's leg." He accelerated slightly and glanced at her from the corner of his eye. "Are you ready for me to shift again?"

Kate gasped and flattened against the back of her seat when she realized where second gear was going to land him. "Don't you dare . . . " Too late. His hand was snug against the center seam of her jeans. He stopped at the corner, shifted into first, and then back to second. His hand was hooked around the knob on the gearshift, and one fingertip secretively pressed into the soft flesh between her legs.

Kate made a strangled sound and squirmed helplessly as the finger insistently stroked against denim that was fast becoming warm and moist. When he moved to third she had to grit her teeth to resist the temptation to grab his hand and put it back where it had been. "Is this bingo place far from here?" she managed to ask.

"Nope," Elsie said. "It's right around the corner."

Kate didn't know if she was relieved or disappointed.

Dave smiled in the dark. "Isn't this fun? Aren't you glad you decided to come?" he asked Kate.

She leveled a look at him. "I think that conclusion is premature."

"Only because this ride was too short." He parked and pulled her out on the driver's side. "If you're especially nice to me tonight, I'll drive all the way home in second."

"You'd better be nice to *me*, or I'll put Elsie in the middle going home."

Fifteen minutes later Kate found herself seated at a table with twelve bingo cards spread in front of her. "I can't do this," she hissed to Dave. "How am I supposed to keep track of twelve cards?"

He looked dumbfounded at his own array of cards. "Elsie says this is the way you do it."

The man on the stage of St. Matthew's auditorium called out "B two."

Kate's eyes frantically moved over all her B's. A thrill of excitement ran up her spine when she located a B2. "I've got one."

"Shhh," Dave said, "you're ruining my concentration."

"G nine. G number nine."

"I've got one of those too!" Kate shouted.

Dave turned and looked at her. Her eyes were bright and her cheeks flushed. The tip of her tongue was caught between her teeth as she waited for the next call. She had a chip ready in her hand. Bingo fever, Dave thought. She was practically rabid with it. He put a few chips on his card to make it look as if he were playing, and he sat back and watched Kate. She'd completely tuned him out again, but he was beginning to get used to it. She was simply a single-minded person throwing every ounce of energy into the task at hand. He thought of the one night they'd shared and decided it was definitely a desirable character trait.

Her hand flashed across the table with another button. "I twenty-six," she murmured.

Elsie was behind her. "This here's criss-cross bingo. You need that zero up in the corner to win. Or you could win with N thirty-seven on the middle card."

The man on the stage called out, "N 14," and a woman across the room shouted, "Bingo."

Kate's mouth dropped open. "How could she get bingo so fast? She must have cheated."

"That's Tootsie Anheiser. She plays with more cards than you. She's a bingo junkie. Drives a school bus all day just to support her bingo habit."

"How awful," Kate said, clearing her cards.

"Yeah. It's sad." Elsie looked over her shoulder as a new game was begun. "Okay, now we're playing whole-card bingo. You gotta fill up a whole card to win this one."

Kate rubbed her hands together and cracked her knuckles. "I'm ready."

Elsie caught Dave's eye. "I'd hate to see her at a racetrack. She'd be running along the rail ahead of the horses."

At eleven o'clock everyone filed out of the auditorium into the cold night air. Kate took a deep breath and looped her arm through Dave's. "All right, now what do we do? I won twelve dollars! Let's blow the whole wad on pizza."

"Past my bedtime," Elsie said. "I gotta get my beauty rest, or I won't be able to make any of them grease burgers tomorrow."

Dave grinned down at Kate. "We can drop Elsie off and do whatever you want."

Kate unconsciously hugged against him. "I want a pizza. Double cheese, pepperoni, onions, green pepper, sausage, and mushrooms. And I want to drive," she said, giving Dave's arm a squeeze. "I've never driven a flashy car like this."

If she'd asked him for the moon, he'd have tried to get it for her. Tomorrow he'd buy her a Porsche. Hell, he'd buy her three to make sure she got the color she wanted. And if she smiled at him like that one more time, he'd go sailing over Washington like a helium balloon. There was real hope for them. Any woman who could get so excited over winning a bingo game could understand the value of Etch A

Sketch. He handed her the keys and walked around to the passenger side, thinking they might name their firstborn B16.

Elsie was waiting for him. "Go ahead and get in," she said.

He bowed in courtly fashion. "After you."

"The hell with after me. I'm not sitting with that gearshift stuck between my legs. I'm an old lady. I've got some dignity."

Kate was already behind the wheel. She blew the horn. "Come on, you two, stop arguing and get in."

He was a man who read comic books, and he knew when the Acme safe was about to score a direct hit on Wile E. Coyote. He heard it now, whistling in the air above his head. He'd been had. He climbed onto the console and tried to stay calm while the engine purred to life. Nothing to worry about, he told himself. It's a short ride. How bad could it get? But he felt sweat break out at the small of his back as he watched Kate's hand curl around the gearshift knob. He sucked in his breath when she skimmed the inside of his thigh with her knuckles en route to first, and he bit back a grunt when she brought the car up to 20 mph and slammed into second with the swift expertise of a formula-one driver. He stole a quick glance down and wondered how well Elsie could see in the dark. Kate shifted to third, and before she could downshift for the corner, Dave replaced her hands with his. "You drive. I shift."

"Party pooper."

"When we're alone you can party all you want."

She parked the car in front of her house and waited while Elsie got out. "Would you mind if I gave you a raincheck on the pizza? I'm starting to fade."

Dave shifted in his seat so he could see her better. "Cold feet?"

"You bet."

"We don't have to party. No more than you want."

"Thanks." She touched his hand. "I had fun tonight."

"Fun is important. You need to have more fun."

"I have fun all the time. I have fun performing."

He relaxed against the car door. "There's all kinds of fun. Some fun is more fun than other kinds."

She laughed. "That's so profound."

"Maybe what we should do is make you a Potato. Can you throw a football?"

"No. And I don't want to throw a football. I think the game is dumb."

Dave sprang off the door. "Dumb? How can you say that? Football is practically the national sport. Football is essential to a well-balanced society. Kate, this is Redskin country."

She wrinkled her nose.

"That does it. I can see I've got to take charge here. You don't like football because you don't know anything about it. Tomorrow I'm going to take you out and teach you how to pass the old pigskin."

"No, no way, never, not me, unh-unh. I'm not the athletic type. I'll break something."

"You mean like a window?"

"Like a bone."

Dave held her hand. "That's ridiculous. We'll just toss it back and forth. Let you get the feel of it."

"I don't have time."

"We'll do it during a break in your practice schedule. We can play in the middle of the street here. It'll be good for you. A little exercise. A little fresh air."

It sounded harmless enough, she thought. It might be nice to get out of the house for a few minutes and play catch with Dave. "Okay. Tomorrow afternoon, around one o'clock. But don't expect much."

Seven

The electricity was back. The roof was fixed. The second floor's ceiling was whole again, and Elsie had been moved up to the third. Everything was back to normal. Nice and quiet. So quiet you could hear a pin drop. It should have been a wonderful day to practice, Kate thought, but she couldn't get into it. Impossible as it seemed, she missed the noise and the activity. She missed Mark and Roy Orbison. And she felt deprived, sitting in her kitchen with her face to a wall. Not to mention the ultimate distraction. David Dodd. He practically *haunted* her. Sleep was impossible; her instant coffee was tasteless and unsatisfying; she couldn't get within three feet of a gearshift without getting a rush, and the clock was inexorably ticking its way to her football lesson. She sighed and leaned on her cello. She should never have agreed to the football lesson. She was going to make a fool of herself. Worse than that, it was time spent with the Enemy. David Dodd inspired sloth and indulgence. He was a bad influence. And he was so darn tempting!

She gave a snort of disgust, grabbed her cello by the neck, and dragged her chair into the living room so she could sit beside the window. She was doing this because of the sun, she told herself. The light was better for reading music. It was not because she could see the street from her perch. After all, she had self-discipline.

While she was rearranging the music, a small bird in the dogwood tree distracted her. The bird was nutshell-brown with a perky black cap and black bib. It twitched its tail and chirped and cocked its head at Kate, looking right at her with its bright black eye. Kate stood immobile, not wanting to frighten the bird away, and suddenly she had an exciting idea. She could hang a bird feeder on her dogwood, and then she'd be able to sit at the window and watch the birds. . . . She hit her forehead with her fist. What a dunce! She was supposed to be practicing. A bird feeder was exactly what she *didn't* need. "Watch the birds!" She groaned out loud and slouched in her chair. She was going down the drain, no doubt about it. And it was all Dave's fault. She hadn't been distracted by birds before he moved next door.

When she heard his front door slam, she knew it was the moment she'd been waiting for all day. Okay, so she admitted it. He was a bum, but she was dying to see him. This morning she'd shaved her legs, put on her best undies, and splashed perfume on her pulse points . . . just in case. Not that she was counting on anything. In fact, she was determined *not* to have anything happen. But just in case . . . Her heart skipped a beat and picked up speed when she saw him standing on her sidewalk. "I hate this," she said in the privacy of her house. "I really hate this." She was infatuated with David Dodd, and she was being sucked into a romance she absolutely didn't want. Despite all her good intentions, she had no control over the rhythm of her heart. It made her furious.

Dave didn't have to read lips to know her mood. Though his smile was hopeful, he gave her wide berth when she stomped down the porch stairs. "So, how'd your morning go?"

"Unh!"

"That bad, huh?"

"I did nothing all morning. You know why? Because of you. You and Mark and Roy and Elsie and that dumb bird who just flew away."

"Mark and Roy?"

"Mark Beaman and Roy Orbison. They're not here anymore, and I keep listening for them."

What a relief. For a minute there he thought he was going to have to duke it out with Mark and Roy. "I could help you out with Roy. I have some tapes—"

"I don't want tapes. I don't want Roy. I want to go back to being the person I used to be. I was happy. I was comfortable." She snatched the football from Dave and wrinkled her nose. "You know, footballs are ugly. You ever take a good look at this thing? It's brown and bumpy. Why don't they make them in prettier colors? And it's shaped funny. It doesn't fit in my hand."

"Maybe we should do this some other day."

She glared at him. "You trying to weasel out of this?"

"Nope. Not me." He adjusted her hand around the football. "See, actually it fits okay if you hold it properly." He stepped back a few paces. "Go ahead. Toss it to me."

The ball went three feet over Dave's head and hit a lamp post. Kate pressed her lips together. "You could have caught that one."

Dave retrieved the football and tried not to grin. Kate couldn't help herself. Bingo fever was mutating. She was a perfectionist, a competitor, a performer. It didn't matter if she was playing the cello, icing a cake, or flipping a football—she played to win. He threw the ball back to her and moved into the road. "This time don't look at the ball. Look at me."

She felt it slide off her fingertips and sail through the air in a graceful arc.

Dave caught it effortlessly. "That's great. You're a natural."

She could throw a football! But she couldn't catch it. He threw it back to her, and it bounced off her head. "You did that on purpose!"

"Pitch it to me and watch the way I catch it. And remember when you throw you look at me, but when you catch your eyes never leave the ball."

"All right!" she said when she caught the next throw. "This isn't bad. Watch me chuck it to you. Watch me roll out for the pass. Watch me . . . *oooof!*" She tripped over the curb and crashed into her garbage can.

Dave waited a minute to see if she'd get up. "Are you hurt?"

"Yes."

He walked over to her. "Are you hurt bad?"

"Yes."

He bent down. "Where?"

"Everywhere."

"No place special?"

She propped herself up on her elbows. "My leg. My right leg."

"Can you move your foot? Can you stand?"

She made an attempt and sucked in her breath. "No. Damn!"

"All right. No reason to panic. You stay there. Don't move, and I'll be right back." He returned with scissors and cut her jeans off above the knee so they could see the leg.

"Well, at least there aren't any bones sticking out," she said, thankful she'd shaved her legs. "Now what?"

He took his keys from his pocket and unlocked his car. "Now we take you to the hospital to get an X ray."

Four hours later they arrived home in a limo.

Elsie rushed out the front door, peered into the car, and put her hand to her chest. Lord, I thought somebody'd died. What are you doing in this thing?"

Kate pointed to the huge white cast on her leg. "I broke my leg and I couldn't get this plaster monstrosity into the Porsche, so Daddy Warbucks rented a limo."

"How'd you break your leg?"

Dave passed the crutches to Elsie and helped Kate out of the car. "We were playing football, and she tackled a garbage can."

"She don't look too happy about it."

Dave paid the driver. "She's mad because I made her cancel all her lessons for today."

Kate grabbed a crutch and stuffed it under her armpit. "And then he called the orchestra and told them I was confined to my bed!"

"The doctor said she has to keep her leg elevated for four or five days." Dave handed the crutch back to Elsie and scooped Kate into his arms.

"Put me down!"

"Soon as I get you into the house."

Kate wriggled. "You're going the wrong way."

"I'm taking you to my place. It'll be easier to take care of you there."

"No!"

"Yes. I was the one who forced you to play football, and I'm the one who's going to nurse you back to health."

"Elsie, do something. Are you just going to stand there and let him kidnap me?"

"Sure," Elsie said. "Dave, am I still invited to dinner on Saturday?"

Dave carried Kate up the stairs and balanced her on his knee while he opened the door. "You bet. Four o'clock." He swung Kate inside and closed the door with his foot.

"I thought you'd invited my parents for dinner on Saturday."

"I did." He took Kate upstairs and set her on the couch. He brought a pillow from the bedroom, put it on the coffee table, and gently laid her foot on the pillow. "I invited Elsie too."

"Ohmigod."

"Nothing to worry about. I told Elsie this was high-class stuff, and she should leave the gun at home." He put a cassette into the VCR and zapped it on.

"*Raiders of the Lost Ark*?"

"This is classic. This is terrific. I must have seen this a thousand times."

Kate grimaced. "Isn't this the movie where they get covered with spiders?"

"Yeah. There's a lot of good stuff in here. Poison darts and booby traps and a bunch of scary chase scenes. You stay put, and I'll go make us some supper."

She rested her head against the back of the couch and closed her eyes. He was trying very hard to be nice to her, and she appreciated it. But she wasn't the sort of person who felt comfortable being waited on. And already she couldn't stand sitting anymore.

How was she ever going to get through four days of this? The bottoms of her feet itched to get moving. Her fingers felt cramped. She looked at the cast and cringed. It was ugly and awkward and wasn't designed to support a cello. Disaster, she thought, this was a disaster. No, wait a minute. A cholera epidemic was a disaster. Starvation in Africa was a disaster. This was just a broken leg. Not even a bad break according to the doctor. A crack in the tibia. No big deal. She'd put on a long dress and nobody'd know. In the meantime she'd watch Indiana Jones do his thing. Except for the spider part. She didn't want to watch the spider part.

Dave sidled into the room with a trayful of food. "Why do you have your eyes closed?"

"I don't want to see the spiders. Are they gone yet?"

"Yeah. If you don't open your eyes you're going to miss the part where he snatches the idol." He set the tray on the coffee table and sat beside Kate. "So, you don't like spiders, huh?"

"I can live without them."

"Spiders are okay. They eat bugs. They catch flies and mosquitoes. Besides, I have it on good authority that the spiders in Raiders are fake."

"They were big and ugly and there were a lot of them."

Dave grinned. "We could watch a different movie. . . ."

"No. This is fine." She looked at the plates of food.

"How did you get all this food? Homemade lasagna, Italian bread, salad."

"Leftovers from the freezer brought to you thanks to the miracle of the microwave. Except for the salad."

"You like to cook?"

He shrugged. "I can take it or leave it. Mostly I like to eat. That means I have to do some cooking."

Kate tasted the lasagna. "It's good. I've never paid much attention to cooking or eating. I've always taken my appetite pretty much for granted."

"Not me," Dave said. "I'm really into appetites. Some more than others, of course."

Kate giggled. "Of course."

He buttered a piece of bread. "You ever get lonely over there in that empty house?"

"Not lately. The loneliest period of my life was when I was married to Anatole. Being alone is different from being lonely, you know."

Dave stabbed a chunk of tomato. "Ever think about getting married again?"

"Never." Liar! This morning she'd written "Katherine Dodd" in the dust on her bureau. "Almost never," she amended. "How about you? Would you like to get married?"

Dave chewed his bread while he thought about it. "Okay."

"Okay what?"

"Okay, I'll marry you."

Kate sat with her fork poised in midair. "When I said would you like to get married, I meant it as a question, not as a proposal."

"Sounded like a proposal to me. And the answer is yes."

"Sure is refreshing to find a man with a sense of humor."

There was just the slightest hint of laughter deep in his eyes. "I'm serious. And you'd better watch your step, or I'll sue you for breach of promise."

She knew he was kidding. At least she was practically positive he was kidding. Still, she felt uncomfortable. Writing names in the dust was one thing—an engagement, even a bogus engagement, was something else. "Is there any dessert?"

He put the empty plates on the tray and stood. "Changing the subject?"

"Marriage talk makes me uneasy."

"No reason to duck the issue." The laughter spread from his eyes to the corners of his mouth. "Marriage is like riding a horse. You fall off and you get right back on and try again, and again, and again."

"Like crashing into garbage cans. Just because I broke my leg this time doesn't mean I should stop crashing into garbage cans."

"Yup. You have to keep doing it until you get it right."

"About dessert . . ."

He returned in a few minutes with bowls of chocolate ice cream loaded with every imaginable topping. "I didn't know what you wanted, so I gave you everything."

"Marshmallow, strawberries, walnuts, chocolate sauce, whipped cream, a glob of butterscotch, and sliced bananas. This is very creative."

"I'm a creative kind of guy."

Kate dug into the ice cream. "You should do something constructive with all that creativity. Isn't there anything you want to do besides play with trains?"

"I like to draw." He reached across her and took a box of crayons from the end table. "I bought myself a new box of crayons today. Not just any box, mind you. This is the forty-eight-crayon size. That's the best size to get. The bigger box has a crayon sharpener, but I like the shape of this box better. It feels substantial in your hand. He popped the top and stared happily at the crayons. "New crayons are great. All perfectly lined up in their paper wrappers, with their little flat tops. And I love the waxy smell." He sniffed appreciatively and held them out to her. "Here. I'll give them to you, and then you'll have something to do while you watch TV. I have a new pad too." He took a pad from the end table and set it on her lap with the crayons."

"Oh, I don't think—"

"It's okay. I'll get myself another box."

Kate stiffled a giggle. She felt silly with her gloppy bowl of ice cream and brand new crayons. All she needed was a pair of patent leather shoes—the kind with the little strap that buckled across the instep. Of course, she wouldn't be able to put them on because her cast wrapped around the bottom of her foot. "What kind of pictures do you draw?"

"All kinds. Mostly cartoons. I always planned to be a cartoonist when I grew up."

"So you're planning on growing up, huh?"

He set his bowl on the table and put his arm around her. "I'm pretty grown-up already."

"Mmmm, well, don't grow up too much. I have a cast on my leg."

He took the spoon from her hand and fed her some ice cream and chocolate sauce. "The cast doesn't cover any of your important parts."

"Watch your step, Dodd. Just because we're engaged doesn't mean you can take liberties."

"Too late. I've already taken all your liberties." He licked a spot of chocolate sauce from the corner of her mouth. "But I'm happy to hear you admit we're engaged."

She took the spoon from him. "I'm not admitting to anything, and you're melting my ice cream."

He drew a line from her knee, up the inside of her thigh. "Remember the gearshift . . ."

Remember it? Only down to the most minute detail. She wriggled away from him. "Stop that! Behave yourself or I'll hit you with my crutch."

He pulled her back. "Your crutch is downstairs in the kitchen."

"Oh, yeah." Kate sighed. He was getting to her. And his fingers were doing clever things at the base of her neck, making her feel relaxed and friendly, making her remember the night they'd spent together. "I don't want to hit you anyway."

His thumb stroked lazy circles up toward her hairline. "That's encouraging."

He didn't know *how* encouraging, she thought ruefully. She loved him, and she wanted to be with him. There were times, like tonight, when she didn't care about motivation and long-term compatibility. There were times when she simply wanted to enjoy the moment. She'd worked hard all her life, and now her leg was broken, and she was forced to alter her life-style for a while. Maybe she should make the most of it . . . just for a day or two.

His voice was soft. It whispered through her hair when he spoke. "Now that you've decided not to hit me with your crutch, are there any other aggressive tendencies we could explore?"

"Mmmm. I think I'd rather make love to you. Very slowly. Very thoroughly," she said.

It was what he wanted too. Very slowly. Very thoroughly. That was the way he kissed her, and that was the way he continued to kiss her while his hand moved just as slowly and just as thoroughly. When she was completely naked, except for the thick white cast, and desperately aroused from the feel of his mouth on every part of her body, he made love to her while she was seated on the big leather couch, with her leg still propped on the coffee table. They'd begun playfully and progressed with gentle expertise, but there was none of that left now. Only passion, raw and hard and demanding. His hands slid under her buttocks, took possession and hauled her to the edge of the couch. He was kneeling between her parted legs, and he thought she was the most glorious thing he'd ever seen. Milk-white skin, swollen pink nipples, and copper red curls that were moist with love.

Her eyes were feverish and wild from desire as she watched him enter her, felt herself stretch to accommodate him. His hands grasped her at the waist and held her firm while he took long, tormenting strokes, lifting her away, unable to breathe when she rode him back. He heard her cry and felt her contract around him, and seconds later he followed her into oblivion.

She looked at him with half-closed eyes and smiled as her pulse rate began to slow. "This is obscene."

"I'm never getting rid of this couch. I might have it bronzed . . . eventually." He put his hand to his heart. "Maybe I should take out more medical insurance."

"It was good, huh?"

He reached for the box of crayons, took the red, and drew a small line on her cast.

When Kate awoke in Dave's bed on Saturday morning the lines tallied up to fourteen. Dave took a green crayon from the nightstand, smiled in happy exhaustion, and crosshatched number fifteen.

"This is a big day," he said, yawning. "Mom's coming today."

"Are you sure?"

"Yup. It's Saturday."

She sat up in bed. "What happened to Thursday and Friday?"

"Thursday we had an Uncle Scrooge festival and spent the day in bed, reading comic books. And

Friday we spent the day in bed seeing how many marks we could make on your cast." He lay spread-eagle under the down quilt. His hair was mussed, and he had a three-day-old beard. "I think I lost five pounds. I need a day off."

"You didn't sound like that an hour ago."

"I wanted to go down in a blaze of glory."

"You succeeded."

He rubbed the stubble on his chin. "Do you think your parents would notice if I didn't shave?"

"Mmmm. I've been meaning to speak to you about that beard. I've got beard rash in a bunch of very tender places. I can't imagine what it's going to feel like when I try to put clothes on."

"You weren't complaining about it an hour ago."

"It's hard to think straight when you're filling me with your glory." She swung her cast over the side of the bed. "Saturday! I haven't practiced in three days. How could this have happened?"

"Tell you what. I'll go next door and get your cello, then you can play some heavy-duty stuff for me while I make breakfast."

An hour later he was frying French toast to Bach. "That's pretty nice," he said. "Do you know any Beatles tunes? Maybe some Police?"

Kate improvised "Eleanor Rigby."

"All right! Now you're playing music." He saw the look of horror on her face and grinned. "Only kidding. I think Bach is okay too."

They both turned at the sound of light rapping on the window of the kitchen door. It was Howie and his partner.

Dave opened the door. "Just in time for breakfast."

Howie looked at the French toast and groaned. "You know what my wife made me eat this morning? Plain yogurt, six ounces of orange juice, and a sawdust muffin. She weighs my food! She has this little scale, and she weighs every lousy morsel of food. She checks my pockets for candy wrappers, and she smells my breath when I come home at night to see if I've eaten pizza."

Howie's partner held out his hand to Dave. "Ed Slikowsky. Everyone calls me Slik. Howie's doctor told him to loose ten pounds, and since Howie's been on a diet he's gained three."

"It's hormones," Howie said. "It's not my fault."

Dave set two extra places at the table. "Coffee?"

Howie nodded. "We have a favor to ask. Remember how you said next time we should shoot from your house and leave the chopper at home? We'd like to take you up on it."

"Something big due to happen?"

Howie sipped his coffee. "Maybe. Your bedroom window is at the perfect angle to keep an eye on things."

"How long do you think you'll be here?"

Howie had his eyes glued to Kate's French toast. She poured syrup over it, and he held his mug in a death grip. "If everything goes as planned, we'll make our move tonight. They're supposed to sell some syrup . . . I mean some dope." He pressed his lips together. "That's real maple syrup, isn't it? Not the fake kind with corn syrup and coloring, but the real stuff that costs $4.75 for a little bottle. . . ."

Dave stacked up a tower of toast, loaded it with melted butter and poured syrup over it until there was a substantial pool of brown liquid in the bottom of his plate. "You've got to get a grip on this diet business, Howard. All it takes is a little willpower."

"Better watch it, Dave. I'm carrying a gun. I'm a desperate man these days."

Dave forked French toast into his mouth. "What you need is more exercise."

"Is that how you do it? You look like you lost weight since I saw you last. In fact, you look like hell. You have bags under your eyes. You need more rest."

Kate cleared her throat to avert the laughter that was bubbling in her chest, and kept her eyes on her breakfast.

Howie looked from Dave to Kate, and a blush rose from his shirt collar. "Oh."

Slik pushed away from the table. "I'll go get the equipment."

"Mostly photographic," Howie explained.

Dave didn't look happy. "I'm having a dinner party tonight—"

Howie held up a hand. "No problem. You'll never know we're here."

Slik returned with a video camera, a tripod, a walkie-talkie, and two shotguns. "Nice of you to let us use your house like this. We'll be real careful not to break anything."

Dave finished his French toast and poured more coffee. Slik's promise not to break anything didn't exactly fill him with confidence. He had an unpleasant vision of his house riddled with bullet holes. "This isn't going to get violent, is it?"

"No way. It's a plain old stakeout," Howie said, refilling his mug. "You mind if I take this upstairs with me?" He stopped in the hallway and called back. "What are you having for dinner?"

"Pot roast, mashed potatoes, steamed broccoli and pineapple upside-down cake for dessert."

Howie thunked his head against the wall. "Oh, God, I love pot roast, mashed potatoes, steamed broccoli and pineapple upside-down cake."

Kate put her plate in the dishwasher, pulled a chair away from the table, and positioned her cello between her legs.

"Does the cast bother you?" Dave asked.

"Yes, but I'm ignoring it."

He sat back with his coffee and watched her. Her hair sprang from her head in big orange curls and framed her face in unruly tendrils. Her eyes were intense as she read the music. Her mouth was mobile, reflecting the passage she played. She stopped and swore and started again. This time her mood was more reflective. She was analyzing problems. She made a mark on her page with a pencil and began again. Even Dave could hear the difference this time. She was settling in. Phase two. He was beginning to know her. When she was learning something new she thrashed around until she got a handle on it, then she mellowed out while she perfected her technique, and when she felt she'd achieved the necessary expertise, she poured energy back into it. He was more of a plodder, he decided. Maybe that's one of the reasons he found her so fascinating. She was constantly changing, varying her intensity.

Kate looked up from her music and was surprised to find him staring at her. "Are you still here?"

"I live here."

"Yes, but don't you have anything to do? Don't you have to bake a cake or something?"

"I wanted to watch you for a while. You're so beautiful when you make music."

She didn't know what to say, just as she was often overwhelmed after making love. It was the same feeling of being complete. Ultimate satisfaction. Gentle euphoria. He loved her. It was in his voice, in his eyes, in the way he touched her, in the way he teased her. No man had ever loved her like this, and she felt as if her whole body were smiling. "Thank you." It sounded dopey, so she blushed.

He wanted to grab her and hug her and never let her go, but he took a deep breath instead. "You're welcome. And you're right. I have a cake to bake."

Eight

Kate's parents arrived promptly at four o'clock. Her mother was slim, dressed in an elegant navy suit with a pink silk shirt. Her brown hair was cut short, showing off chunky gold earrings and a face that was pretty despite her look of apprehension. Kate's father was a brick of a man: sturdy Irish stock. He was square-faced with tightly curled red hair and Kate's green eyes, although they'd faded somewhat with age. He was medium height and heavy-boned. And he shook Dave's hand as if he were weighing a melon that was several ounces short of expectation.

"Nice to meet you, sir," Dave said.

"I understand my daughter's living with you."

Dave gauged the arm span on Michael Finn and took a precautionary step backward. "She broke her leg, and it was easier to care for her in my house."

Kate swung in on her crutches. "You aren't going to grill Dave, are you?"

Michael Finn smiled at his daughter. "Of course I'm going to grill Dave. Fathers are supposed to do things like that. Isn't that why we were invited to dinner?"

Grace Finn walked into the living room. "Look, dear, Dave has furniture. And it's nice. It's not all black leather and chrome." She bent to admire an earthenware jug of fresh-cut flowers. "These are lovely."

There was another knock at the door, and Dave let Elsie in.

"Man," Elsie said, "it's gonna snow. It's colder'n a witch's . . . um, nose out there."

Dave took Elsie's coat, but she insisted on keeping her big black patent leather purse. "Never like to be too far from my purse," she explained to Kate's mother. "Never know when you're gonna need a hanky."

Kate looked at Dave and rolled her eyes. They both knew what was in the purse.

"Elsie," Dave said, "I thought we'd agreed that you should leave your hanky at home today."

She took a seat in the wing chair with her purse on her lap. "I thought about it, but when I picked up my pocketbook and slung it over my arm, it just didn't feel right. Never know when you might need a hanky."

Kate plopped herself in the other wing chair and stretched her leg out on an ottoman.

"What are those marks on your cast?" her mother asked. "Do they mean something? They look like crayon."

Kate stared stupidly at the tally lines.

"Toe exercises," Dave said. "She's supposed to do toe exercises every day, and it's hard to keep track of them, so we mark them on her cast." Did they buy that?

Elsie shook her head. "Boy, you must think we're really dumb. Toe exercises, hah."

"That's an awful lot of marks," Kate's father said to Dave. "Didn't anybody ever tell you about moderation. You want to pace yourself, son. You'll get a heart attack." He drummed his fingers on the padded arm of his chair and didn't seem displeased at the idea of Dave biting the big one.

A dark blush stained Dave's cheeks. "I feel fine, sir. Honest."

"You look like hell. You've got bags under your eyes."

"I've been busy."

Michael Finn's eyes narrowed. "I just bet you have."

"Daddy!" Kate glared at her father in warning.

Mr. Finn leaned forward in his seat. "You must make a good salary to afford a house like this, Dave."

Dave loosened his tie and popped the top button on his shirt. He needed *air*. "Actually, I bought this house with my lottery winnings."

Michael Finn digested that. He sat silent for a moment and then resumed his drumming. "I'm not a gambling man myself."

"Oh." Stay calm, Dave told himself. This isn't as bad as it seems. It couldn't possibly be. "That's admirable, Mr. Finn. Keeping a tight rein on those vices, huh?"

"I believe in hard work," Mr. Finn said. "You get something through hard work, and you appreciate it."

Dave was beginning to better understand Kate. Her father was obviously a man who'd brought himself up through the ranks and was proud of his accomplishments. Because he'd instilled those same work ethics in his daughter, it was difficult for her to respect rewards that were too easily won. And he suspected there had been little room for play in the Finn household. Play would be equated with goofing off.

"So exactly what sort of job do you have?" Michael Finn asked Dave.

Dave had known it was coming. The old Acme safe. Baboooom! "Well, sir . . ." It wasn't that he was ashamed or embarrassed by what he did, Dave thought. It was that no one ever seemed to fully understand. "I don't exactly have a job."

"Oh?"

"I guess you could say I'm self-employed."

Slik ran down the stairs and stopped short at the living room. "Oops. Hello," he said, obviously surprised to find everyone watching him.

Dave held his breath. Now what? Could it get any worse? "Some friends are doing a little photographic work upstairs," he told Mr. Finn. "It's of a technical nature."

"Yup. It's technical all right. Sorry to have intruded," Slik said, backing away. "Need to get a piece of equipment from the car."

Elsie squinted after Slik. "Something familiar about him."

Kate felt her heart flop in her chest at the thought of Elsie impulsively blasting away at Slik's privates in front of her mother. That would be a migraine to last a lifetime. And Slik wouldn't like it either. Yessir, the cloud of doom was sliding over Dave's house. It was only a matter of time. After tonight, breaking her leg was going to seem insignificant. "You've probably seen him in the café," Kate said. "Probably seen him with Dave. They're . . . friends." She looked Elsie straight in the eye. "Dave wouldn't like it if anything happened to Slik. Would you, Dave?"

"No." Dave shook his head vigorously. "I wouldn't like it at all."

Kate put her finger on her left eyelid to stop the nervous twitch she'd suddenly developed. "Now that we have that settled, I think we need some refreshments. Anybody want wine? Daddy, you need a beer?"

Michael Finn looked at the bottle Dave handed him. "Imported. Just how much did you win in that lottery?"

"Five million."

"That's a lot of money," Mr. Finn said. "Investing it?"

"Uh, no. Not yet. So far I've just been spending it."

Grace Finn caught the look of incredulity on her husband's face and, without even realizing what she was doing, drained her glass of sherry. Her eyes opened wide, and she clapped her hand to her chest. "Goodness," she gasped.

Slik returned with what was obviously a rifle wrapped in his suit jacket. He nodded politely to Kate's parents and hurried up the stairs.

Elsie gave a long, low whistle. "Damned if that didn't look like a rifle."

"I don't think so," Kate's mother said. "It wasn't a rifle, was it?"

Michael Finn just raised his eyebrows.

"Tripod," Kate said. "That's my story, and I'm going to stick to it, so don't anybody bother asking questions."

Elsie leaned forward in her chair. "Something's going down. I can smell it."

"Nonsense." Kate forced a thin smile and cracked her knuckles. "That's pot roast you smell. Dave, could I see you in the kitchen a minute?"

"Excuse us," Dave said. "We have to check the pot roast and stuff."

Kate propped herself against the refrigerator and closed her eyes in a moment of unguarded desperation. "I just want you to know that no matter what happens tonight . . . I love you."

Dave grinned down at her. "It's not so bad."

"No?"

"No. I think your mother likes me. And your dad hasn't punched me out yet."

"He's showing a lot of restraint. They're really not bad people." She was distracted by a group of men running through Dave's backyard. "Why are there men running through your yard?"

"They looked like cops. Probably just taking a shortcut."

"I guess I'm being silly, huh? Worrying about nothing."

He kissed her on the nose. "Everything's going smoothly."

Kate cocked her head. "Was that a gunshot?"

He lowered his mouth to hers. She'd said she loved him. Sort of a strange admission of love, but he'd take it. "Want to tell me again that you love me?"

She wrapped her arms around his neck, and the crutches clattered to the floor.

"What was that?" Elsie yelled. "Something break in there? That wasn't more gunshots, was it?"

"Kate accidentally dropped her crutches," Dave called, kissing Kate again. "I'm not up to another notch on your cast, but it would be nice to cuddle. Maybe we could tell everyone to leave."

Kate wanted to cuddle, too, but she didn't think asking her father to leave without supper was a good idea. "I think it would be wise to feed them first." She stiffened in his arms. "Do you hear police sirens?"

"Probably some cop late for dinner."

"On our street? We don't have any cops living on

our street." Her voice had risen to a pitch just short of a dog whistle. "Give me my crutches!"

Howie came bounding down the stairs three at a time and passed Dave on a run. "We need the bullhorn from the car! We need the tear gas!"

Dave stood at the open back door. "Couldn't you wait until after dinner?" he asked hopefully.

Howie returned with his arms full. He stopped in the middle of the kitchen and sniffed. "Oh, man, that pot roast smells great. You have little onions and carrots cooking with it?"

"Yeah." Dave lifted the lid. "Looks good, huh?"

"You going to make gravy?"

"Sure. You have to have gravy with pot roast and mashed potatoes."

Slik shouted from the top of the stairs. "Howie, you got the stuff? Would you hurry it up down there?"

Howie swore under his breath. "Sometimes this job's a pain in the butt."

Kate felt as if she'd fallen down the rabbit hole. Howie Berk was counting his tear gas canisters while he discussed gravy with Dave, and her mother and Elsie were sitting side by side in the living room, getting skunked on sherry, speculating on the size of Slik's gun. Kate thumped her way into the living room and tried to look calm. "How's it going?" she asked. "Anybody need more wine?"

Elsie and Grace Finn held out their glasses.

"Looks to me like we got a drug bust going," Elsie said. "Looks to me like we got feds upstairs." She patted her purse. "Good thing I brought my hanky with me."

Dave refilled Elsie's glass. "You so much as *touch* your hanky, and I swear I'll beat you senseless with Kate's crutch."

"Hah!" Elsie said. "You and who else?"

"*Me*, that's who else," Kate said. "You don't want to mess with a redhead."

Elsie pressed her lips together. "You got a point."

"Drug bust?" Kate's father looked out the window. "Is that true? What kind of neighborhood is this?"

Dave shook his head. "This is a great neighborhood. Really quiet. Very respectable. I'm sure this isn't a drug bust."

From the second floor the walkie-talkie sqwaked and there was the sound of glass breaking. "Okay," Howie yelled over the bullhorn, "we know you're in there, Omar. Come out with your hands in the air." There was a moment of silence, and then the bullhorn was directed down the stairs. "Sorry about the window, Dave. We couldn't get it open. Next time don't paint over the latch."

"I could be wrong about the drug bust," Dave said. "But I'm sure it's not important. Probably just some kid smoking in his bathroom. You know how the police always overreact."

Grace Finn slugged down another glass of sherry, and Kate rushed to refill her mother's glass.

"Mom, don't you think you're drinking that sherry kind of fast? You're not much of a drinker, you know."

"Don't worry, dear. I've only had one eensy-teensy glass."

"Mom, this is at least your third glass!"

Dave stared at the blue and red flashing lights outside his house. Grace Finn had the right idea. He'd like to get drunk, too, but he had to mash the potatoes, and he made it a point never to operate machinery while under the influence. He cautiously set a bowl of salted nuts at Mr. Finn's elbow and backed away. "Guess I'd better mash the potatoes now."

Kate pivoted toward him on her crutches. Her eyes were as big as golf balls, and she spoke in a rapid-fire shriek. "You need help in the kitchen?"

"Sure. You know CPR?"

A SWAT team assembled on the front porch and the Evening News van double-parked in front of Kate's house.

Elsie got to her feet. "You look kind of pale," she told Dave. "He's a nice kid, but he's kind of a wimp when it comes to shooting people," she said in an aside to Kate's mother. "Hasn't lived in the right sort of neighborhoods." She turned her attention back to Dave. "How about if I give you a hand with those potatoes?" She tucked her purse under her arm and marched off to the kitchen. "The key to good mashed potatoes is to add just the right amount of milk," she explained to Kate. She drained the potatoes and added a blob of butter and some milk. "Some people use a potato masher, but I like an electric mixer."

Dave took the pot roast from the Dutch oven and set it on a platter on the table. He closed the kitchen door and felt much better. Out of sight, out of mind, he told himself. "I'll make the gravy, and, Kate, you can get the broccoli going."

"Broccoli," Kate said, a vacuous glaze settling over her eyes.

Shouts rang out from the alley behind Dave's house, and the back door flew open. A man burst through the door and stopped in the middle of the kitchen. He was young, in his early twenties, and desperate-looking. He made a subtle movement with his hand and the gleaming blade of a knife flashed.

"Well, if this don't beat all," Elsie said, hands on hips. "What do you think you're doing busting in here like that."

He pointed the knife at her. "Shut up, you old bat, or I'll make you look like Frank Perdue's package of chicken parts."

"Old bat?" Elsie's eyes narrowed. She whipped the .45 out of her purse and leveled it at the man. "Drop that knife or I'll blow your eyeballs clear out of your head. And back off from the pot roast. I don't want you ruining my dinner."

Howie ran into the kitchen with his pistol drawn, and two uniforms came through the back door.

"You're a little late, Howie," Dave said, waiting for his heart to start beating again. "Annie Oakley already nabbed him."

"Sorry. He slipped away from us and made a run for it." Howie looked at the gun in Elsie's hand and muttered an oath. "You have a permit for that monster?" he asked Elsie.

Elsie, Kate, and Dave all answered in unison. "Absolutely."

Howie made a disgusted sound. "Put it back in your pocketbook. I'm gonna pretend I never saw it."

Kate's mother staggered into the kitchen. "Michael found a portable TV on the end table and tuned in to the football game. You don't mind, do you, cutie pie?" she asked Dave.

"Hell no," Dave said, stirring his gravy, and feeling a little hysterical, barely able to keep from laughing. "How's the game going?" he yelled to Mr. Finn.

"Notre Dame's ahead by seven."

"Good!" he called back. "That's good, isn't it?" Dave asked Kate.

Kate giggled. "Makes my day a lot better." Her mother was practically drunk. Her father thought Dave was a bum. And their pot roast had been caught in the middle of a police raid. The word *disaster* hovered at the forefront of Kate's mind.

Dave read her thoughts. "And we haven't even eaten yet."

"We're going to look back on this someday and think it's pretty funny."

He put his arm around her and kissed her on the neck. "Your mother called me cutie pie!"

Elsie left at eight and Kate's parents left at eight-thirty. Kate and Dave stood on Dave's front porch and waved good-bye.

"That went pretty well," Dave said, rolling his eyes.

Kate rested her head on his shoulder. "My father said if I married you, he'd put me up for adoption, and it's the first time I've ever seen my mother drunk."

"She wasn't *real* drunk. She was just a little . . . tipsy."

"She dropped her roll in the gravy boat and fished it out with her fingers!"

Dave pressed a kiss into her hair. "I liked it when she buttered her thumb."

They turned and went into the house, sealing the world off with the click of the dead bolt.

He circled his arms around her in the foyer. "Remember when we were in the kitchen, and you told me you loved me?"

"Mmm-hmm."

"Would you tell me again?"

She leaned into him, pressing her breasts against the wall of his chest, and she kissed him deeply. "I love you," she whispered into his mouth. Her tongue touched his and she repeated the phrase. "I love you."

Sunday morning Kate awoke, looked at Dave asleep next to her, and silently admitted she loved him beyond reason. She'd admitted it to herself, to Dave, and to her parents. Now what? A couple years earlier it would have been simple. Go with the flow. Live with him, marry him, divorce him if it doesn't work out. But that was a couple years earlier. She was older and wiser now. She didn't want to live with a man outside of marriage. In her eyes it lacked commitment. It was irresponsible. She bit her lip and acknowledged that she'd been doing just that. She was in Dave's bed and had been there for four nights. And what about marriage? There was a time, not long ago, when she'd vowed she'd never again get married. Now she wasn't sure. But she was dead sure of one thing. She'd gotten her last divorce. If she ever married again, it would be for keeps. The next man would be chosen much more carefully—she knew more about what she needed in a relationship now. And she knew Dave lacked some of the qualities she wanted in a husband. "Damn."

Dave flopped an arm over her. "Something wrong?"

Kate sighed.

He opened one eye and looked at her. "That was an awfully big sigh. You're not still worried about your mother, are you? She'll be fine. She probably doesn't even remember sliding off her chair."

"We need to talk."

"Okay."

She made a dismayed sound when she felt him stir against her. "This is serious!"

"I know. I think I have terminal lust."

"Maybe it would be better if we did this at the breakfast table."

"That's a little kinky, but I'm game if you are."

Kate swung her cast over the side of the bed. "I meant talk!"

"We could do that too."

She pulled on a pair of sweats that had been cut

off above the knee and dropped a sweatshirt over her head. "I need coffee."

Dave groggily glanced at the clock. Six-fifteen. Groan. Why did she always have to be up at the crack of dawn? "Be right with you," he said. Three hours later he opened his eyes and knew he was in big trouble. He dressed in the first thing he found lying on his bedroom floor and plodded down the stairs to an empty house. She'd made coffee and drunk it, and she'd finished off the pineapple up-side down cake from the night before. Her crutches were gone. Her cello was gone. The light of his life was gone. He stuffed his feet into a pair of white court shoes and went next door.

" 'Morning," he said when Kate answered the door. "Are we living here now?"

Kate examined him from head to toe. His hair hadn't been combed, he needed a shave, his shoe-laces were untied, and she was positive he wasn't wearing any underwear. He was adorable . . . but he was a slob. She'd already showered, put in two hours of practice, and called almost all her private pupils. The best she could say about Dave was that he was on his feet. She shook her head. "How can you stand to waste a morning like this?"

"I'm not a morning person. Why did you leave?"

She'd left because she couldn't stand him sleeping upstairs while she was pacing downstairs. She knew it was stupid, but it infuriated her to be working her buns off trying to perfect Suite 5 while Dave had his face smashed into a pillow. "This isn't going to work."

"No?" What the devil was she talking about?

"We're just too different."

"Un-huh."

Kate tipped her nose up a fraction of an inch and pushed on. "I need a man who's more . . . conventional."

"I'm conventional. I don't have any tattoos. I wear oxford cloth buttondowns when I go to a restaurant. I live in a house."

"You don't have a job."

"I don't need a job. I'm rich."

Kate studied her feet. "I don't think I can live with that."

"You have something against money?"

"No. I like money. I just don't think I could live with a playboy. I'm a very motivated person. I feel uncomfortable living with a man who's not equally motivated."

Dave followed her into the kitchen. "I'm motivated."

"Sex doesn't count."

He opened the refrigerator door and helped himself to a carton of orange juice. "Oh, now that really hurts."

"Dave, you don't *do* anything. You play with toys all day. You read comic books."

"I like toys and comic books. That doesn't mean I don't enjoy other activities. I read the paper. I read best sellers. I read cereal boxes." He poured himself a glass of juice and drank it. "You underestimate me. You think I'm just another pretty face."

"Okay, so you read cereal boxes. What else do you do?"

"I draw cartoons."

Kate sat on a straight-back chair and tuned her cello. "I mean what *real* things do you do?"

"Cartoons are real."

"We aren't making much progress here. Our personality types are too different. I'm type A, and you're type . . . I don't know if you have a type."

"I don't see why this job stuff is so important. Seems to me if you loved me, it wouldn't matter what I did for a living."

"It's because I love you that it matters. I don't want to mess up your life with a relationship that's doomed from the start."

He raked his hand through his hair. "Hell, don't you think it's a little late for that? Don't you understand . . . I don't have a life without you."

Kate clenched her teeth and swallowed back the tears that were burning in her throat. She found she couldn't talk, so she played. Bach. Suite 5. It was awful. She concentrated on the sheet music, but the notes were waving in front of her. She blinked away the tears and attacked the opening passage. When she finally looked up, he was gone.

Kate got out of the cab, swearing. She stuffed her crutches under her arm and looked contemptuously at the cello case sitting at the curb. "Great. Just great. How am I going to get this thing into the house? She would have asked the cab driver, but he didn't speak English. Elsie. No. Elsie would still be at bingo. Dave. He was the only one left. "Damn!" She swung her crutch at her garbage can, lost her balance, and fell flat on her back. *"Dave!"* No response. *"David Dodd!"*

Dave ambled down his steps and stood over her. She was wearing her long black velvet dress and black velvet cape, and she was stretched out in a pool of lamplight. "Why are you lying on the sidewalk?"

"I fell."

"I suppose you want me to pick you up."

Kate gritted her teeth. "That would be nice."

"Haven't seen you in a couple of days."

"Are you going to help me up, or what?"

Dave rocked back on his heels and crossed his arms loosely over his chest. "I don't know if I should. You kicked me out of your life."

"Anybody ever tell you that you have a mean streak?" She saw the smile flash across his face and felt her heart stop. Lord, she loved him! How'd she ever get herself into this mess?

He drew her to her feet and dusted her off. "You have a concert tonight?"

"Sort of."

"Why are you home so early? It's only nine o'clock."

She narrowed her eyes, whirled around on her plaster-encased foot, and hobbled toward her house. "I don't want to talk about it."

Dave picked up the crutches and the cello case and followed after her. He took her key, opened her door, and then carried her up the stairs. "Everything has its price. I picked you up, and now you have to tell me all the awful details of the evening." He turned on the light and looked around in surprise. "You have furniture."

"The real estate lady said it would help to sell the house. Besides, I have students coming over here for lessons now. The students' mothers need a place to sit."

He untied the narrow velvet bow at the neck of her cape and let it slide from her shoulders. Her dress had a low neck, ending where the swell of her breast began. The dress hugged her slim waist and the curve of one hip before falling to the floor in a full skirt. Around her neck she wore a cameo on a velvet ribbon, and her cameo earrings matched. Classy, Dave thought. And very sexy. He stuffed his hands into his pockets to keep from running his finger along the neckline. "Sounds like you're getting your life in order."

Kate winced at the pain behind his eyes. She'd hurt him, and she couldn't make it better. The knowledge was almost worse than her own misery. "Sometimes good things come out of bad things. I can't drive, so I arranged to have my students take their lessons here. I don't know why I didn't think of it before. It saves me a lot of time, and I don't have to brave the traffic." An awkward silence stretched between them. He wasn't going to make this easy, she thought. He was going to quietly stand his ground and make her come to him. He had good instincts, she decided. He knew if he didn't push, she'd resume the friendship. But that was as far as it would go. Friendship. She smoothed an imaginary wrinkle from her velvet skirt. "Would you like a cup of coffee? I bought a coffee maker."

"Coffee would be nice."

He watched her swing off to the kitchen on the crutches and thought they looked incongruous with the elegant black gown. She must have been a sight onstage at the Kennedy Center with her bare toes peeking out from the white plaster. She wasn't long on common sense, but you had to respect her dedication.

She leaned one crutch against the counter while she filled the coffee maker with water. "I'm not up to grinding my own beans yet, but I got a special blend at the deli."

"Better be careful or before you know it, you'll be cooking."

Kate snorted. "That's one way to kill time on your hands."

Dave leaned back in a kitchen chair. "You have time on your hands?"

"I've been given six weeks sick leave. I'm not to come back until my cast is off."

"Does this have something to do with your foul mood?"

Kate's shoulders sagged. She might as well tell

him. He was going to pry it out of her sooner or later. "Things didn't go as smoothly as I'd anticipated."

"How rough was it?"

"I trashed the entire string section."

"Didn't mess with the brass, huh?"

"Well, yes, actually some of the brass went too."

Dave's eyes were wide. "You did this onstage?"

"Of course I did it onstage. What do you think, I ran over them with my car in the parking lot?"

He'd seen her drive. She could do it. "Anybody help you accomplish this feat?"

"Nope. Did it all by myself."

"Don't suppose you'd want to tell me the gory details?"

She took a bag of cookies from the small pantry and set it on the table. "We were filing in and I accidentally stomped on the bass player's foot with the stump of my cast. He shouted out this really rude word and pulled his foot out from under me. I guess it was understandable. By the time I left, the guy's toe looked like an eggplant. Anyway, I lost my balance and grabbed for his arm, but I only snagged his sleeve. The sleeve ripped clean off his tux, and I went face first into the string section . . . in front of a sell-out audience." She grimaced. "It was awful. A whole row of music stands went down like dominoes with sheet music flying all over the place. It took a half hour to straighten out the music and restore order."

Dave almost strangled on swallowed-back laughter. "Um, that doesn't sound too bad."

"That's not all."

"What else did you do?"

"It took three people to get me up on my feet. And it was all very confusing, what with the doctor onstage looking at the bass player's toe, and people milling around, bending over to pick up music. And I . . . I accidentally goosed the first clarinetist with my bow." She chewed on her lower lip. "They tell me I got more laughs than Joan Rivers."

"Hey, it could happen to anyone."

"You think so?" That was a hopeful thought. She'd hang on to that.

"What happened after you goosed the clarinetist?"

"The conductor escorted me off the stage and called a cab, personally! I don't blame him. Actually, he's very sweet, and he was worried about me." She sat down carefully in the seat opposite him and folded her hands on the table. "So I have a vacation." She tried a smile, but it wobbled on her face. "I'm not sure I know what to do with a vacation."

Dave covered her hands with his and gave them a squeeze. "You'll figure it out. You'll have time to do more practicing. And you can sit in the audience once in a while and get a different perspective." He grinned. "You can go to bingo every night with Elsie."

The coffee was ready, but she didn't want to move. Her hands felt good under his. This was exactly what she needed. Support, comfort, and warmth. David Dodd wasn't stingy with his emotions. And he knew how to grin and tease her out of a funk. He might not be the perfect marriage prospect, but she doubted she'd ever find a better friend. She mustered up a reasonable amount of bravado. "Bingo with Elsie doesn't sound half bad. And you know what else? I'm going to hang a bird feeder on my dogwood tree!"

"That's pretty radical."

"What the hell, I may as well go all out on this vacation thing."

He wanted to propose a real vacation to her. A trip to the Bahamas or a week in the Florida Keys, but he knew she wasn't ready for that—yet. So he poured out two cups of coffee, helped himself to a cookie, and tried not to smile too broadly. The image of Kate knocking over an entire row of music stands was enough to set him off howling, and the idea of her on forced vacation had his heart skipping beats. Katie Finn, he thought to himself, you don't stand a chance.

Nine

Elsie looked at Kate and shook her head. "Pitiful," she said. "You've been on vacation for three days and already you're blimping out."

Kate dropped the stick from her Fudgsicle into the empty potato chip bag and sighed. "I'm not blimping out. Besides, how could you tell? All I ever wear are these sweats. You can't tell if someone's blimping out in sweats."

"You got a double chin."

"Water retention."

Elsie grunted. "Too much salt from all them chips you eat."

Kate pinched her chin between her thumb and forefinger and decided it didn't feel fat. Elsie was exaggerating. So she ate a few chips. Big deal.

"And them game shows you watch all day are

gonna rot your mind. Don't you have anything better to do than to watch game shows? Why don't you
play your cello? Look at it . . . it's got dust on it."

"It doesn't have dust on it. I practiced for two
hours this morning."

"I heard that practice. You were playing 'Row, Row,
Row the Boat.' "

Kate turned her attention to the window. "Elsie,
you ever notice there aren't any kids in this neighborhood?"

"Yeah. Spooky, isn't it? It's a lot like being in the
old people's home, except this here's yuppie heaven."

"What do you suppose would happen if someone
got pregnant on this street? Think everyone else
would get up a petition to make her move away?"

Elsie gathered empty glasses and soda cans and
carted them off to the kitchen. "Nobody's gonna get
pregnant in this neighborhood. Nobody has time.
Everybody's too busy making money and eating bean
sprouts."

"Dave isn't too busy."

"Dave can't get pregnant."

Kate continued to stare out the window. "No, but I
could."

"The hell you could. You're not married. Have you
been careful?"

"I haven't had to be for the past week. I haven't
seen Dave."

"He took you out to dinner last night."

Kate searched her pockets for a candy bar, finally

found it, and slowly peeled away the wrapper. "I know, but I haven't *seen* him."

"Yeah, well you're lucky he hasn't seen *you*. You're getting a roll."

"I can't go to my exercise class with this cast on my leg."

"Hmmph. How come you two haven't been *seeing* each other?"

Kate watched a squirrel leap onto the bird feeder and eat all the seeds. "I decided it was best if we were just friends. He's a great person, but we're so incompatible. All he does is hang around the house all day."

"Looks to me like that's all *you* do."

"Yes, but I'm on vacation."

Elsie buttoned herself into her blue coat and slipped her purse over her arm. "Maybe he's on vacation too."

"For six months?"

"It's allowed. He don't look like such a slouch to me. I think he's just getting his ducks in a row."

Kate wondered if that's what she was doing—getting her ducks in a row. She didn't think so. Her ducks had been in a row. Something had happened to all those neat little ducks, and now she couldn't even find them much less line them up. It seemed that every day was a little worse than the one before. Her mind had begun wandering, and she had thoughts of ridiculous things. What color curtains she'd like in her living room; the lasagna she'd attempted to make on Thursday that had turned out perfect;

skiing. She'd never been skiing. Twenty-eight years old and never been skiing! This morning while she was practicing she'd looked down at the cast and fantasized that she'd broken her leg on the slopes. She'd spent an entire half hour on that daydream. "What do you suppose is the matter with me, Elsie? I've turned into a lump."

"I don't know, but I gotta go to work. I'm pulling a double shift today because everybody's sick with the flu. Then after work I got a date."

"A date?"

"Yup. With a real hunk. And he's no old coot either. Doesn't look a day over sixty. Delivers sweet rolls to the café every morning."

"That's kind of romantic." She watched Elsie walk away, and she searched for other activity on the street but found none. The squirrel had eaten all the seeds and left for better pickings. It was Saturday afternoon, but it was too cold for yard work. People came and went, but no one dallied outdoors long enough to be interesting. She clicked the TV off, and the silence of her empty house pressed in on her.

Maybe what she needed was a pet, she decided. A dog would be nice, except dogs had to be walked, and she wasn't so hot at walking these days. And besides, she'd heard a rumor that dogs ate cellos. That left cats, birds, goldfish, hamsters, and guinea pigs. She rested her forehead on the cool window-pane. She was doing it again! She was thinking silliness. A pet! Lord, what would she do with a pet when her life resumed its normal rhythm?

Dave appeared on the sidewalk and waved to her. She felt the smile start in her heart and work its way through her body. She hated to admit how dependent she'd become on him. He helped her navigate stairs, and he chauffeured her around town. And he made her happy. It was the happy part that had her worried. She wasn't supposed to get this excited about someone who was just a friend. Boredom, she told herself. Isolation. It was all taking its toll. It was blowing her feelings about Dave out of proportion.

He let himself in and joined her in the living room. "How's it going?"

"I'm thinking of getting a cat."

It was thirty seconds before he found his voice. "A cat?" His mouth creased into a broad grin. "What brought this on?"

Kate was embarrassed. "I don't know, it sort of jumped out at me. Dumb, huh?"

"No. It's a great idea."

"Well, I was just *thinking* about it."

He twisted a red curl around his finger. "We don't have any plans for tonight. Would you like to check out some kittens?"

"Yes!"

At nine-thirty Kate and Dave struggled through Kate's front door under an enormous burden of boxes and bags and a cat carrier. Kate collapsed on her new couch and swung her leg up on the coffee table.

"I'm never going shopping with you again. You're a maniac! You're a bad influence on me. Look at all the money I've spent!"

"You didn't spend any money. You charged everything."

"That's even worse. How am I ever going to pay for all this? It'll take me years."

"No, it won't. You're going to marry me, remember? I'm rich."

She leaned her head back and closed her eyes. "That was a joke."

Dave took the tiny black kitten from its carrier and set it in her lap. "Not to me it wasn't."

"Dave, we have nothing in common."

He sat beside her and stroked the kitten. "We love each other, don't we?"

It was true. She couldn't deny it.

"And we both like Uncle Scrooge comic books, and we both like freshly squeezed orange juice, and we fit together very nicely." He put his arm around her and cuddled her close to him to prove his point. "See?"

Kate tilted her face toward him for his kiss. "Mmmm. That's all true.'"

"So what's the problem?"

"You've neglected to mention our differences."

He kissed her again. "Nothing insurmountable."

She set the kitten on the floor and stood up to get some distance from him. "You don't know. You've never been married and divorced. *Everything* is insurmountable when you're married. The fact that you want to talk at the breakfast table and he insists on reading his paper is insurmountable. Leaving the seat up on the toilet is insurmountable. Getting peanut butter in the jelly jar is insurmountable. People don't change just because they're married. All those little habits and personality quirks that you previously thought were trivial become the bane of your existence. And the major problems, like different outlooks on life, are crushing."

"No relationship is perfect. You have to weigh the odds and make a decision—"

"Damn right. And our odds are terrible."

Dave felt anger boiling in him. He'd waited a long time to fall in love, and just his luck it had to be to an obstinate redhead. "You're running scared from Anatole and not looking clearly at what we have going for us."

Elsie opened the front door with her key and stood at the entrance to the living room. An elderly man stood behind her. "Lord," Elsie said, "you can hear the two of you shouting at each other clear out on the sidewalk. Haven't you got anything better to do than to shout at each other?"

Dave relaxed into the couch. "We might do that later. We thought we'd get the shouting out of the way first."

"Sounds like a good plan to me," Elsie said. "This here's Gus. He's taking me out dancing, so I've gotta change my shoes."

Dave and Gus shook hands.

"Nice place you have here," Gus said.

"It's not mine." Dave pointed to Kate."It's hers. I live next door."

Gus looked over at Kate. "Nice place you have here, ma'am."

"So you're taking Elsie out dancing, huh?"

"Yup."

Kate scrutinized him. "You won't be late, will you?"

"Um, I don't know . . ."

"Elsie works the *early* shift, you know," Kate said, putting emphasis on the word *early*.

"Yeah, no kissing on the first date and call us if you can't make the eleven-thirty curfew." Dave rolled his eyes and hooked his arm through Kate's. "Can I see you in the kitchen, please?"

"In a minute. I have a few more questions for Gus."

Dave caught her at the waist, slung her over his shoulder, and carried her away. "Now," he said. "I think we should talk now." He closed the kitchen door and set her on her feet.

"Why did you do that?" she sputtered. "That was humiliating!"

"Kate, you were grilling the poor man. You were about to ask him for credit references. I know that look in your eye. You were going to get his license plate number."

"The first date and he's taking her dancing! I know his type."

"Oh, yeah? What's his type?"

"He delivers sweet rolls!"

Dave put his hand to her forehead. "You feeling okay?"

"You think I overreacted?"

"Just a tad."

"I do that a lot, don't I?"

Dave dragged her against him and held her tight. "Mmmm. You're a hot-headed, hot-blooded wench." He kissed her with exaggerated passion and she started giggling. "What are you giggling about? This is serious kissing."

He could always make her laugh, she thought. He was playful—something she'd never known in a man before. The men in her life had always been on the somber side. She considered Dave and decided she liked this better. Much better. "We're not supposed to be kissing. We're supposed to just be friends."

"I never agreed to that."

Gus tapped on the kitchen door. "We're going now. It's been nice meeting you."

Kate stuck her head out. "Nice meeting you, Gus. Have fun tonight."

"There's a young man came to see you," Gus said. "I sat him down in the living room."

Kate opened the door wider and looked beyond Gus. "Ohmigod."

Dave looked over Kate's shoulder. "Who is that?" he whispered. "He looks like he's made of wax."

"It's Anatole."

"Does he move?"

Kate gave him an elbow. "Of course he moves. And

he doesn't look like he's made of wax. He just has fair skin."

"I've seen people who were embalmed and looked healthier than that."

"You aren't going to make a scene, are you?"

"Wouldn't think of it."

Anatole looked healthier at close range. With his fine skin and well-defined features he was Hollywood's image of a Russian aristocrat. He had pale blue eyes, perfectly coiffed blond hair, and professionally buffed fingernails. His face was virtually expressionless. When Kate approached him, he stood as a formal posture of respect and uttered an indiscernible word of greeting. He completely ignored Dave.

Dave grabbed Anatole's hand and pumped it. "David Dodd. Nice to finally meet you, Anatole. Kate's told me so much about you."

Anatole raised his eyebrows slightly. "Oh?" He looked at his hand, still in Dave's, and a definite expression formed on his face. Annoyance. He squeezed Dave's hand a trifle harder than custom called for and repeated Dave's name in a voice laced with condescension. . . . "David Dodd. What a quaint name."

Dave returned the squeeze and locked eyes. "Kate thinks so. She's going to be using it soon. Katie Dodd. How does that sound?"

"Sounds like a bird call," Anatole said, tightening his grip. The muscles of a body builder rippled under his suit jacket, and a red flush began to creep from his starched shirt collar.

Cords stood out in Dave's neck, but his arm didn't

waver. His eyes narrowed, and his biceps bulged within the confines of his blue flannel shirt.

Anatole's face had turned brick red. His lips compressed into a grim smile as he took a wider stance and put weight behind strength.

Dave grunted and applied increased pressure. "So, you're an ohhh-bow-ist, huh?" The words crept from between his teeth.

A vein throbbed in Anatole's forehead. "I'm the best."

"The hell you are." Dave accidentally on purpose stepped on Anatole's soft-as-butter Italian loafers.

"Stop it!" Kate shouted. "This is the most disgusting display of macho crud I've ever seen."

Anatole dropped Dave's hand and stared open-mouthed at his scuffed shoe. "He stepped on my foot!"

"It was an accident," Dave said.

"That was no accident. You deliberately stepped on my foot!"

Kate pushed Dave aside and faced Anatole. "Did you want to see me about something special? Or is this just a social call?"

Anatole plucked a huge basket of fruit from the floor. It was wrapped in orange cellophane and had a big lavender bow attached to the handle. "I was deligated to deliver the traditional basket of get-well fruit. And I'm supposed to tell you Ralph is almost able to get a shoe on his foot, and everyone misses you." He gave Kate an antiseptic kiss on the cheek. "Poor Kate. How have you been?"

Dave took a deep breath and willed himself to concentrate on the fruit basket. The thought of Kate married to this pompous, egocentric excuse for a man had his stomach in a knot. Count oranges, he told himself, calm down. There were four oranges in the basket.

Anatole squinted at a flash of movement in the dining room. "I don't want you to panic, Kate, but there's something running around in your dining room. Something small and black."

"That's my kitten."

Anatole's reaction would have been exactly the same if she'd said that's my pet rat. "You also have a boarder."

"Yup. Elsie. She's terrific."

Anatole looked at Kate's stomach. "Pregnant, too, I see." He lowered his voice. "I know you've always wanted children, but don't you think you could have been more discerning about a father? In fact, marriage isn't even necessary these days. There are a lot of single-parent families."

Kate clapped her hands to her stomach. "I'm *not* pregnant! This is water retention." She stared down at herself and sighed. To be honest, this is Ben and Jerry's Brownie Bars. She glanced at Dave and saw the flicker of surprise pass behind his eyes.

"I didn't know you always wanted children," Dave said, looking incredibly pleased by his discovery.

"It was a phase," Kate said. "A very brief phase. I had this ridiculous notion that I could handle a concert career and motherhood all at the same time.

But, as you can see, I can barely find my own socks in the morning. There are some women who simply weren't meant to be mothers."

"That's okay by me," Dave said. "You can be the father. I'll be the mother."

"He's a little weird," Anatole said to Kate. "He isn't dangerous, is he?"

Kate smiled. "He has his moments."

She'd barely gotten the words out of her mouth when the house was rocked by a series of explosions. Glass rattled and the street was lit by the orange glow of fire. Dave looked past Kate, through the long, curtainless windows. "It's the drug house across the street!"

Flames shot from every window of the house. Smoke billowed from the roof and began to cast a pall over the neighborhood. People poured into the street from surrounding houses, and sirens screamed in the distance. There was no sign of life in the burning building, but the very thought of it sent a chill through Kate. She hobbled down her front stairs and stood squinting at the spectacle, mesmerized by the power of the fire. It was impossible not to stare at it. It was compelling and horrible and awesome. She could feel the heat against her face and hear the hiss of destruction.

Suddenly a man bolted from the shadows of Dave's cellar door and crashed square into Kate. They sprawled flat on the sidewalk in a tangle of flailing arms and thrashing legs. The man pushed away from her, muttered an oath, and scrambled to his feet. A police car arrived on the scene, and behind the police car a fire truck rumbled to a stop. The man stood frozen, as if suspended in time by the headlights shining directly on him.

He wasn't one of her neighbors, but she'd seen him before, Kate decided. In her kitchen! It was the man with the knife. The man Elsie'd almost blown to smithereens. His panic was palpable, like an animal trapped in the hypnotic glare of a hunter's spotlight.

He looked to the far end of the street and was confronted by more police cars and fire trucks. There were no alleys in between. Each house was attached to the next. He pulled a gun from his jacket and pressed the snub-nosed barrel against Kate's temple. "Get up," he said, wrapping his hand around her upper arm. *"Move!"*

Kate recoiled at his touch, revolted by the odor of sweat and gun oil. She felt her stomach roll and stared at him stupidly. The gun pressed more insistently into her flesh. She struggled to stand but had little luck with the awkward cast.

"Wonderful," he muttered, "I have to pick a cripple to take hostage." He gave a grunt and jerked her to her feet, holding her close. "No one come near me."

"This isn't a good idea," Kate told him. "I'm not so great at walking."

"We don't need to walk. We're gonna get a car. We're gonna use this one that's double parked with the keys in it."

Anatole's mouth fell open. "That's my car!" he whispered to Dave. "Do something!"

Dave narrowed his eyes. "If I do anything, it'll be to rearrange your face."

"Get in the car," the man told Kate.

"My cast won't fit."

"*Make* it fit! Jeez, lady, give me a break. Hang your leg out the window if you hafta." He pushed the seat back as far as possible and shoved her in.

Kate looked over her shoulder. "We're surrounded by police cars."

He fired a shot through the sunroof and leaned on his horn. "You ever have a day when nothing goes right?" he asked Kate. "You ever blow up a building by mistake? All I wanted to do was get some of my equipment back and make a little dope."

"I thought you were arrested when the police raided the house? They caught you in my kitchen."

"I made bail. Man, the trial won't be for months. How do they expect me to make a living until then. I gotta pay lawyers. I gotta buy jurors and judges. They locked all my equipment up. They deprived me of my right to work at my chosen profession."

The police cars pulled back, and he gunned the motor.

Kate braced her hand on the dashboard. "Where are we going?"

"Cripes, lady, how the hell do I know? I thought we'd just ride around until we run out of gas." He maneuvered around a police car and took off down the street.

A 1957 Cadillac flew around the corner and fishtailed down the middle of the road, heading straight for Anatole's car. Both drivers slammed on their brakes and swerved, narrowly avoiding a head-on collision. Kate looked at the driver of the Cadillac and clapped her hand over her mouth. Elsie!

In his haste to avoid Elsie, the gunman had jumped the curb and smashed into a wrought iron fence. He took a deep breath and jammed the car into reverse. Kate looked out the rear window and saw Dave wrench the Cadillac's door open and dive in. The Cadillac spun around and peeled out with a screech of tires. They were coming after them! And behind the Cadillac was a line of police cars. In the dim recesses of her brain she realized if she hadn't been so terrified she would have found it funny. As it was she could barely hold in her hysteria, but her years of performing, enabled her to perform now. She used every shred of self discipline to keep her voice steady when she spoke. "I think we're being followed."

"No joke! Tell me it wasn't a little old lady driving that Cadillac."

"You remember Elsie?"

"Remember her? She would have splattered my brains all over your linoleum. That woman's nuts. She's seen *Rambo* too many times." He looked in his mirror. "I'd give myself up to the cops, but I don't know how to do it without Grandma Moses getting to me first."

"Traffic light!" Kate shouted. "Everyone's stopped for the red light!"

The man stomped on his brakes and pointed his gun at Kate's head. "You see this, Elsie?" he shouted. "You come near me and I'll blow the cripple away." He checked the mirror again and a look of disbelief registered in his eyes. "What is she doing? What the *hell* is that crazy woman doing?" He looked around frantically for someplace to move the car. None. There were cars on every side of him. The Cadillac was closing in fast on his rear—and it wasn't slowing.

The impact jerked him forward and knocked the gun from his hand. Anatole's car bounced forward, crumpling into the car in front of it, but not enough to cause damage to the driver or passenger. Kate held tight by the seatbelt she insisted on wearing heard multiple crashes occurring behind her and saw the reflection of red and blue lights flashing everywhere. Before she could gather her wits, Dave's arms were around her, unbuckling the belt, lifting her from the car, holding her close against his chest. She could feel her heart pounding and then realized it wasn't her heart that was pounding, it was Dave's heart she felt. Uniformed police officers had the gunman in custody. Howie ran forward from one of the cars in the rear and went to the man, making sure his rights were read to him properly.

"I'm okay," Kate said. "You can put me down."

Dave's voice was thick. "I don't think I can. I don't think my arms will let go!"

They both laughed nervously when he set her on her feet, and she grabbed his sleeve for support. "I couldn't believe it when it turned out to be Elsie in the Cadillac."

Dave kept his arm tight around her waist. "Gus has a CB in that boat. They heard the call go out for police and fire and lit out for home. Apparently Gus wasn't driving fast enough to suit Elsie, so she took over behind the wheel." He shook his head. "I think this was the first time she's ever driven a car. She crashed into you because her heel got caught in Gus's rug."

Kate hobbled along the sidewalk and surveyed the destruction. Anatole's car looked like an accordion. Four police cruisers were in various stages of smashed disarray behind the Cadillac. And the Cadillac didn't have a dent.

Gus polished a fender with his sleeve. "She's classic," he said proudly.

Howie ambled over to Dave and Kate. "Who the devil was driving this Cadillac?"

Elsie stepped forward. "I was," she said, her mouth clamped tight, her eyes glittery little steel orbs.

Howie shook his head. "How did I know that?" He looked up to the heavens. "Why me? Why me?"

"Don't you want to know if I have a license?" Elsie asked.

Howie chewed on his lower lip. "No," he said. "I definitely don't want to know if you have a license."

"I have a license," Dave said.

Gus raised his hand. "So do I."

"Good enough for me," Howie told them. "I'm not traffic anyway."

When they finally got back to the house, Anatole was sprawled on the couch, working his way through the fruit basket, watching TV. Dave stared at him in amazement. His shirt didn't have a wrinkle in it, his hair was perfectly in place, his tie not even a millimeter askew. "He doesn't grow whiskers, does he?" Dave whispered to Kate.

"Of course not. Whiskers are messy. They wouldn't dare grown on Anatole's face."

Anatole was on his feet. "My car?"

Dave smiled at Kate. "Let me tell him."

"All right, but you owe me," Kate said.

"Totaled. Smush city. Looks like John Candy sat on it."

Anatole turned pale. "It was one of a kind. Special order. I waited six months for that car."

Dave clucked his tongue in sympathy. "How long have you had it?"

A half-eaten apple rolled from Anatole's hand and dropped on the floor. "Two weeks."

"Boy, that's a shame," Dave said. "Prime depreciation."

Anatole ran his hand through his hair, but nothing moved out of place. "How am I going to get home?"

"Don't worry about it," Elsie said. "I'll give you a lift." Anatole looked defeated, but he followed her outside.

Dave and Kate stood at the living room window and watched Elsie peel away from the curb.

"Anatole deserves it," Dave said.

Kate agreed. "He needs more excitement in his life."

A lone fire truck stood vigil, playing a stream of water on the smoldering remains of the gutted building across the street. The smell of smoke was everywhere, penetrating the houses. Outside Kate's window the truck engine hummed as it continued to pump water. Men called to one another. The truck radio crackled with messages. The flasher on a police car sent pulses of color up and down the street.

Dave wrapped his arms around Kate and kissed her neck. "Now what? Are you hungry? Are you sleepy? Are you sexy?"

"Yes."

"How about if we go over to my house, where we'll have more privacy. . . ."

Kate suddenly felt shaky. She'd used up all her bravery, all her energy, all her self-discipline. She wanted nothing more than to be taken care of, to lie in Dave's arms and feel safe and cosseted. And she wanted to be in a house where she could draw the curtains on the world. "That sounds great. Just let me get a change of clothes from upstairs."

The unopened boxes and bags from her shopping trip had been dropped in a heap by the stairs, and a scratching post and litter box that didn't fit in a bag sat beside the other parcels. Kate went cold at the sight of them. The kitten. She'd forgotten all about the kitten. It had been bounding around in noisy exploration just before the explosion, and now the house was quiet. It hadn't come to greet them. It wasn't anywhere in sight. She tried to remember if they had left the front door open when they'd all rushed outside, and she was almost certain they had.

Dave saw her face turn white and followed her eyes to the litter box. "Oh, damn."

Without saying another word, they began a methodical search of the house. It wasn't difficult. The house wasn't fully furnished. There were few corners where a kitten might hide.

When every nook and cranny had been examined and the kitten hadn't turned up, Kate sat down at the bottom of her stairs and burst into tears. A camera pod had broken through her roof, she'd broken her leg, she'd laid waste a concert, she'd witnessed a rump roast being held at knife point, and she'd been kidnapped. Somehow she'd been able to get through it with a sense of humor and an occasional tremble of her lower lip. But neglecting a kitten was more than she could bear. All her worst fears about herself were true.

Ten

"I'm an airhead," she wailed. "All I know is music. I haven't a scrap of common sense. And I'm totally self-centered. Like Anatole. I should have stayed married to him. We make the perfect pair."

"You're not an airhead. You're intense, and you're dedicated to your music. That doesn't make you an airhead. And you're certainly not like Anatole. You're the precise opposite of Anatole. You're full of life and enthusiasm and joy. You're passionate and spontaneous and loving."

Tears streamed down her cheeks. "I lost my kitten."

"The house across the street exploded! We all ran out to see what was happening. It was as much my fault as yours. Probably more. I don't have a cast to slow me down. I should have checked on the door."

She was inconsolable. "It was *my* kitten. I was responsible for it."

He wiped her tears away with his thumb. "Everything will work out all right. We haven't looked outside yet. Kittens have a way of turning up when they get hungry."

She hiccuped and went in search of a tissue. "That's true. We haven't looked outside." She blew her nose and slowly moved toward the front door on her crutches.

Dave watched the effort she had to exert to keep going, and felt his throat clog with emotion. She was out on her feet, and from the way she gingerly carried her broken leg, he suspected she was in pain. "Kate, why don't you let me look for the kitten?"

"I can't. This is something I have to do."

Damn stubborn redhead, he thought. She was going to make a hell of a wife. He ran next door to get a flashlight and followed her around the neighborhood, calling 'kitty, kitty, kitty' and shining the light in front yards, under cars, into porch corners.

Finally she admitted defeat. Her leg throbbed unmercifully, and she was bone-tired. They'd traveled three blocks in every direction, but there was no kitten. She hadn't even named it, she thought miserably. She'd brought it home and immediately forgotten about it. Now it was lost, or worse. She thought of all the emergency vehicles that had roared up and down her street for the better part of the evening, and a chill shook her. It would have been so easy for a kitten to get caught under one of those huge tires.

When Dave suggested she spend the night with him, she didn't object. She simply wanted to crawl into the first available bed and go to sleep for a very long time. And when she woke up she would go back to her music, just like before. It was the one thing she could count on. She was good at it. She had control. If things didn't go right, only she was hurt.

"We'll look again in the morning," Dave said. "When it's light."

Kate nodded, her eyes bright with tears. "In the morning," she whispered.

He carefully undressed her, buttoned her into a flannel pajama top, and tucked her into his bed. She was hurting, and he couldn't help her. She was too tired to fight back. The best he could do was to comfort. But come morning, when she had some of her normal resiliency, they were going to have a discussion.

Kate woke up with a hangover. Not enough sleep and too many tears, she thought. She didn't feel nearly as desperate as she had the night before, but her head was pounding. She propped herself up in bed and squinted at the sunlight splashing through the open window.

" 'Morning," Dave said, sliding through the door with a tray. "I've brought you breakfast."

"Breakfast in bed. Some special occasion?"

"Its in honor of your foot. It's swollen. Too much activity yesterday."

Kate looked under the covers and confirmed it. "Damn."

He set the tray across her lap. Orange juice, waffles, four links of sausage, and coffee. "I talked to Howie this morning. They're holding your kidnapper without bail, and the fire's definitely out in the house across the street." He nibbled on a sausage. "They're boarding it up until the owner has a chance to start restoration. . . ."

"And no one's seen my kitten."

Dave sighed. "I'm sorry."

Kate looked at her breakfast. "This was really sweet of you, but I don't think I can eat anything."

"You have to have a little faith, Kate. We'll find the kitten."

How could she tell him? It wasn't just the kitten. He was probably right, and the kitten would come out of hiding when it got hungry. Her real problem was Dave. She loved him more than life itself. More than music. More than she'd ever thought possible. He was always there for her. He made her feel fragile and strong and desirable—all at the same time. He knew when to cuddle, when to stroke, when to tease. And he made her feel needed. He made her feel like a necessary part of his life. He would never be someone she simply passed in the kitchen en route to work. Their mating went far beyond the physical. It was emotional and intellectual, as natural as breathing. And just as essential. Thinking about it, having him here on the bed beside her brought so much pain she could hardly speak, because she was firmly convinced they would never get married. Even her father had seen the futility in the relationship. He'd tempered his feeling with fatherly affection and placed the blame on Dave. Kate understood about transference. His judgment was slightly skewed but essentially correct. She and Dave were all wrong for each other. And on top of that, Kate knew she wasn't a family sort of person. She threw tantrums and forgot to make meals and lost kittens. Not mother material. And that was very sad, because Dave was definitely father material. He needed a kid to share his comic books and run his train. Someday he'd find a woman who liked the idea of a rich man lazing around the house all day, and they'd live happily ever after. Kate felt the tears gathering in her eyes and pushed the tray away. She didn't want to tell him about her pain. She'd rather he think it was over the kitten. And in a way it *was* over the kitten. Poor helpless little thing, she thought. She'd loved it from the first moment she laid eyes on it. Just like Dave. The thought of losing both of them was almost more than she could manage.

"It's really important that I find my kitten," she whispered, her voice thick with swallowed-back tears. "I love her so much. How can you love something so desperately when you've known it for such a short time?"

"Sometimes it happens like that," Dave said gently. He touched her flushed cheek with his fingertips and kissed her trembling lips. It wasn't a kiss of passion. It was solace and understanding, love in its purest form. His heart was breaking for her. He knew this wasn't just about a kitten. She was going through a crisis, facing truths about herself, both real and imaginary. And he was going to wait for her to pass through that crisis. He'd wait a lifetime if he had to. He wouldn't be dissuaded by her doubts about their compatibility because he knew they were right for each other. Not perfect, maybe, but close enough. Perfect would be boring. That brought a smile to his lips. Life with Kate would never be boring. "You're too hard on yourself," Dave said. "And you're thinking too much. I'd guess you're a person who usually relies on instinct. What do your instincts tell you, Kate?"

"Are we talking about the kitten?"

"Nope. We're talking about us."

"I don't think I'm up to 'us' talk. Could we do this some other time?"

He kissed her on the forehead. "You bet. I have things to do anyway. You eat your breakfast, and I'll take another look around the block for the kitten."

An hour later she was dressed and slowly making her way down the stairs when Elsie knocked on the door. Kate's heart jumped when she saw the little black kitten in Elsie's arms. "You found it!" she said, throwing the door open.

"Yup. I saw it wandering around in the front yard." Elsie handed Kate the squirming animal.

Kate held it at eye level and studied it. "Elsie, this isn't my kitten. My kitten had one little white foot."

"Shoot," Elsie said. "I didn't think you'd notice."

"Did you actually find this kitten in my front yard?"

"Nope. I bought it at the pet store, and they won't take it back."

Kate set the kitten on the floor and watched it scamper around the dining room. "It's cute. I suppose if we find my first kitten, it would like to have a friend." She gave Elsie a hug. "It was nice of you to do this for me."

"You were pathetic," Elsie said.

Kate found it in her to smile a little. "Would you like a cup of coffee?"

"Nope. I have a date with Gus. I gotta go meet his daughter."

"Sounds serious."

"Yup. I found a winner this time. He's got a nice rent-controlled apartment just two blocks from here. He's perfect."

Now Kate really smiled. "Perfect for what?"

"Perfect for everything. Damned if he isn't."

"Elsie! I hope you're being careful."

Elsie giggled. "I'm being careful to snag him fast. You wait around when you're my age and before you know it, one of you has a heart attack."

The thought of Elsie and Gus together brought a new lump to Kate's throat. Why was marriage so easy for other people and so difficult for her?

When Elsie left, Kate fixed the litter box and gave the new kitten a bowl of milk. She'd just settled down in a chair when her mother and father rapped on the front door. "We called early this morning," her mother said, inching her way into the foyer, "and we heard about your lost kitten." She gave her daughter a hug and a kiss. "Honey, I'm so sorry. Dave said the little thing just vanished into thin air."

Kate nodded and tried not to sniffle. It was hard to be cheery when people kept bringing up the subject of her misery.

"Daddy and I know it must get lonely for you sometimes, and so . . . well, we got you a new kitten."

Her father took a fat black kitten out from under his topcoat. "It's black. Just like your old one. We went to every pet store in northern Virginia and two in Maryland before we found a black kitten," he said proudly.

Kate looked at the kitten. "Is it returnable?"

"You don't like it?" Kate's father looked crushed.

"I love it. It's just that Elsie had the same idea." Kate shrugged and smiled. "Oh, what the heck. You never have too many kittens." She took the kitten from her father and cuddled it.

"Your father has something else to say too," Kate's mother said, giving her husband an elbow in the ribs.

A sheepish smile lit Michael Finn's face. "I was wrong about Dave. I think he's okay. He really loves you." He shrugged. "And maybe if you nag him enough, he'll get a job someday."

Kate heard the front door thrown open and turned to see Dave bustle in.

"Look what I've got!" he said, holding a bedraggled black kitten aloft.

"My kitten?"

"No. I couldn't find your kitten, so I went to the animal shelter, and I adopted an orphan. I got there just in time. They were going to gas this poor little tyke." His mouth dropped open when two more black kittens ran across his feet.

"One's from Elsie and the other's from my mom and dad." Kate smiled. "Everybody loves me."

Dave put his kitten on the floor to join in the fun. He went to Kate and kissed her tenderly. "I know I sure do."

Kate looked at him solemnly. She loved her kittens, but she knew nothing was ever going to replace Dave. She was going to hang on to all these wonderful little loving moments, she decided. She was going to remember them when she was old and lonely and unloved. A tear trickled down her cheek. "PMS," she told her mother and father. "I'm fine . . . really."

Kate and Dave had just finished saying good-bye to Kate's parents when a taxi pulled up to the curb and Anatole got out. He had another orange and lavender fruit basket. Dave met him at the door.

"I ate all your fruit last night," Anatole explained. "So I thought I should replace it."

Dave took the basket for Kate. "Thanks, Anatole. That was nice of you."

Anatole recoiled at the sight of three black kittens bounding down the porch stairs. "It's a herd of cats!" he said. "Wasn't one enough? Isn't there a law against having more than one?" He looked at them more closely. "Where's the original? The one with the white sock."

"Lost," Dave said. "It was missing when we came home last night, and we can't find it anywhere."

Anatole seemed puzzled. "You mean it got out of the backyard?"

"What?"

"Didn't you find my note?"

Dave and Kate answered in unison. "No."

"The kitten was running around looking frantic, and it occurred to me that it might be needing a cat bathroom, so I put it out back. I made sure the back gates were locked, so it couldn't get out."

Dave smacked his forehead with the heel of his hand. "I never thought to look in the backyard."

"I left you a note in the kitchen . . ." Anatole said, but Dave and Kate had already rounded up the kittens and disappeared inside the house with them. Anatole held his finger aloft, made a circular motion with it indicating the international gesture for fruitcake, and climbed back into the cab.

'It's in the backyard!" Dave shouted to Kate. "Anatole put it in the backyard!"

He opened his back door and the kitten tumbled in. It looked up at him and meowed. Dave burst out laughing. "She's hungry."

Kate couldn't believe her eyes. She scooped the kitten up and held it close.

"Now why are you crying?" Dave asked in total exasperation.

Kate didn't even try to stop the tears. "I'm so happy!"

Dave took four bowls from the kitchen cabinet and filled them with cat food. "Women," he said gruffly, and when he turned back to Kate his eyes were bright.

Kate let out a long, slow breath. Never in a million years would she have suspected it could be like this. Loving someone so much that their pain was your pain, and their joy was your joy. That's how much Dave loved her, and that's the love she returned. She bit her lower lip and gave her head an almost imperceptible shake. She'd been incredibly stupid. She'd almost thrown away the love of a lifetime because Dave didn't fit into her silly preconceived husband mold. She went to Dave and wrapped her arms around his neck. "You like me, huh?"

He nodded his head.

"And you're happy the kitten's been found?"

He nodded his head again.

Kate kissed him tenderly. "I think I finally figured it out. I thought my marriage to Anatole failed because of irreconcilable differences, but I was wrong. It failed because we didn't love each other. We never loved each other. At least not the way husbands and wives are supposed to love. Our marriage is going to last forever because the differences between us won't matter so much. You were right. It's our love that's important."

It took him a minute to find his voice. "You're a pretty smart lady."

"It took me a while."

He kissed her slowly, savoring every moment of it.

"I'm glad you decided to marry me. I'd hate to think of these kittens growing up illegitimate." He leaned away from her just a bit so he could better look at her. His eyes were serious when he finally spoke. "You're going to make a good kitten mother."

"Because I love them too?"

"Yup."

"If I had some help, I might even make a passable child mother," she said, smiling. "Don't you think?"

"You'll make the best child mother ever. And we'll make sure there's room in your life for your cello."

She thought she might bubble over with happiness. She had everything she'd ever wanted. And it was going to get better. Every year with Dave would be better than the one before. She felt his heart beating against hers and was overwhelmed with emotion. Mine, she thought. My husband, my lover, the father of my children. It was exciting. Her whole life was expanding before her very eyes. She was going to continue her music, but she was going to find time for other things as well. She might never learn to actually bake a cake, but she was going to learn to throw a football. She might get a dog, she decided, so the kittens would have something to torment. She'd definitely have a baby. She wanted a house that was filled with noisy love and activity. She could buy houseplants now because Dave would remember to water them. And she was going to get sexy underwear . . . maybe a garter belt. After all, she would be young only once, she told herself. Live it up.

She rubbed against Dave and ran her hand along the curve of his neck. "Is that crayon still on the nightstand?"

"You mean the crayon we use to record your toe exercises?"

Kate's fingers found their way down to his waist, popped the snap on his jeans, and wiggled their way through layers of clothing until they found smooth skin. She smiled when she felt his stomach muscles tense, heard the quick intake of breath. "I have an urge to . . . do toe exercises," she said, letting her finger stray lower and lower.

Dave was breathless. "If that finger goes a half an inch farther south, you're going to be doing toe exercises on the kitchen floor."

Kate pulled away in mock horror. "Not in front of the kittens!"

He grabbed her behind the legs and carried her out of the kitchen, up the stairs to his bedroom.

Kate held tight to his neck. "Are you being romantic or are you being nice to my injured leg?"

"Neither. I'm getting you into my bed in the fastest way possible."

And that's the way they undressed each other— fast. But when it came to making love, it was slow. His hand and his mouth skimmed every surface, finally settling in on the most tender, the most erotic. And when she ultimately received him, it was to seal the contract they'd already made. Their eyes locked in affirmation of their love, and they began the rhythm that would sow the seeds of their marriage.

Almost instantly the rhythm took over, and what had begun as a spiritual joining turned to a struggle to survive the passion that ripped through them. Their affirmation had unleashed the last vestiges of restraint. Their need was desperate. She dug her fingers into his sweat-slicked back and clung to him, arching into each thrust, almost delirious with desire each time he bore down. She didn't know how it could continue, but it did, until the fire licking at her was unbearable and the deep aching thrum of sex was all-consuming. Nothing else existed. Only the awful pleasure. He drove himself into her, deep and hard, and they cried out together—unintelligible sounds of deliverance and love.

Later that afternoon Dave studied what was left of the crayon. "Look at this poor thing," he said. "It's worn down to practically nothing."

Kate studied the new marks on her cast and smiled in contentment. "We need a fresh crayon."

"They're all upstairs."

Kate propped herself up on one elbow. "I've never seen your third floor. You always keep that door locked. Just exactly what have you got up there?"

Dave toyed with a red curl that curved around Kate's earlobe. "It's sort of a . . . studio."

Her curiosity was aroused. "What kind of studio?"

Good question. He didn't know what kind of studio. It was a little bit of everything. It was his junk drawer. But it had its serious side too. "I guess it's some kind of artist's studio. Mostly it's just a bunch of stuff." *All my favorite things,* he privately added. *The equivalent of your cello.*

Kate struggled to get out of bed and began a hunt for her clothes. "I'd like to see it. I've always wondered about that locked door. Why do you keep it locked?"

Dave sighed. "Because I was afraid if you saw what I have up there, you'd be even more convinced I was all wrong for you." He followed her in the clothes search, gathering together underwear and socks.

It seemed silly now, but Kate knew it might have been a real concern two days earlier. She realized that she'd been on a witch hunt of sorts, looking for reasons to justify her fear of marriage. Fortunately Dave was a patient man. And a wise one. She watched him puzzling over a third sock he'd found and couldn't resist the urge to tease him. "What on earth have you been hiding, dismembered body parts?"

"Worse than that," Dave said, zipping his jeans. "Toys."

Kate's eyes grew wide. "More toys?"

He took a key from the top dresser. "They help me to think. I know that sounds crazy, but they sort of get me in a mood." He led the way to the attic door and unlocked it. "Some of them are pretty special. Collector's items. Most of them are just fun."

Kate crept up the stairs behind him and blinked in amazement. Not in her wildest, most childish fantasy could she have imagined anything like this.

Huge skylights had been cut out of the back half of the roof, splashing sunlight over most of the room. The remainder was lit by recessed lighting. There were games, books, bubble-gum machines, weather vanes, toy trucks, a basketball hoop. . . . It was a seemingly endless collage of colors and textures. She was sure it was the happiest, coziest nest anyone ever built. And in the middle of this riot of indulgence was a sturdy, no-nonsense drawing board. A small rolling set of shelves sat beside the drawing board. It held pencils, pens, brushes, crayons, Magic Markers, erasers, rulers, and some sort of mechanical device.

"What's this?" Kate said pointing to the machine.

"Airbrush."

"What do you do with it?"

"I draw cartoons." He went to the drawing board and flipped a half-finished page for her to see.

She stared at the figures running across the frames. "This looks familiar."

Dave smiled. "That's because you're finding time to read the funnies in the paper these days."

"This is a great cartoon," Kate said. "This guy here is from outer space, and he fell in love with a crossing guard named Patti. . . ." She looked at the drawings in front of her. "Why are you copying these cartoons?"

"I'm not copying them. I'm *drawing* them."

Kate looked at the signature in the last frame. *David Dodd.* "You really draw this? You mean you thought of it and you get paid for it?"

"Yup."

"Why didn't you tell me?"

"I did tell you. You weren't listening. Every time I said I drew cartoons you'd roll your eyes and say, 'Yes, but what do you really do?'"

Kate felt her stomach drop away. He was right. "I feel like a complete jerk."

Dave hugged her to him and chuckled. "It wasn't all your fault. To tell you the truth, I was a little insecure and was just as happy to keep it a secret for a while. It's been syndicated for only three weeks. Initially it was for a one-month trial, but it's become so popular they've offered me a long-term contract. And I'm negotiating a comic book contract for it too." He held her at arm's length, and the concern showed in his eyes. "Do you really like it?"

"I love it! And I love your room. I can see where it would inspire you to write comic books."

"You think you could practice your cello here?"

Kate laughed. "No. I need someplace that doesn't hold so many distractions."

"We have a problem, Katie. We need a bigger house."

Kate agreed. "We need a house in a family neighborhood," she said. "Someplace where there are children skipping rope in driveways. Someplace with *lots* of bedrooms."

THE EDITOR'S CORNER

This month our color reflects the copper leaves of autumn, and we hope when a chill wind blows, you'll curl up with a LOVESWEPT. In keeping with the seasons, next month our color will be the deep green of a Christmas pine, and our books will carry a personalized holiday message from the authors. You'll want to collect all six books just because they're beautiful—but the stories are so wonderful, even wrapped in plain brown paper they'd be appealing!

Sandra Brown is a phenomenon! She never disappoints us. In **A WHOLE NEW LIGHT,** LOVESWEPT #366, Sandra brings together two special people. Cyn McCall desperately wants to shake up her life, but when Worth Lansing asks her to spend the weekend with him in Acapulco, she's more than a little surprised—and tempted. Worth had always been her buddy, her friend, her late husband's business partner. But what will happen when Cyn sees him in a whole new light?

Linda Cajio's gift to you is a steamy, sensual romance: **UNFORGETTABLE,** LOVESWEPT #367. Anne Kitteridge and James Farraday also know each other. In fact, they've known each other all their lives. Anne can't forget how she'd once made a fool of herself over James. And James finds himself drawn once again to the woman who was his obsession. When James stables his prize horse at Anne's breeding farm, they come together under the most disturbingly intimate conditions, and there's no way they can deny their feelings. As always Linda creates an emotionally charged atmosphere in this unforgettable romance.

(continued)

Courtney Henke's first LOVESWEPT, **CHAMELEON,** was charming, evocative, and tenderly written, and her second, **THE DRAGON'S REVENGE,** LOVESWEPT #368 is even more so. J.D. Smith is instantly captivated by Charly, the woman he sees coaching a football team of tough youths, and he wonders what it would be like to tangle with the woman her players call the Dragon Lady. He's met his match in Charly—in more ways than one. When he teaches her to fence, they add new meaning to the word touché.

Joan Elliott Pickart will cast a spell over you with **THE MAGIC OF THE MOON,** LOVESWEPT #369. She brings together Declan Harris, a stressed-out architect, and Joy Barlow, a psychologist, under the rare, romantic light of a blue moon—and love takes over. Declan cherishes Joy, but above all else she wants his respect—the one thing he finds hardest to give. Joan comes through once more with a winning romance.

LOVESWEPT #370, **POOR EMILY** by Mary Kay McComas is not to be missed. The one scene sure to make you laugh out loud is when Emily's cousin explains to her how finding a man is like choosing wallpaper. It's a scream! Mary Kay has a special touch when it comes to creating two characters who are meant to be together. Emily falls for Noble, the hero, even before she meets him, by watching him jog by her house every day. But when they do meet, Emily and Noble find they have lots more in common than ancestors who fought in the Civil War—and no one ever calls her Poor Emily again.

Helen Mittermeyer begins her *Men of Ice* series *(continued)* with **QUICKSILVER**, LOVESWEPT #371. Helen is known for writing about strong, dangerous, enigmatic men, and hero Piers Larraby is all of those things. When gorgeous, silver-haired Damiene Belson appears from the darkness fleeing her pursuers, Piers is her sanctuary in the storm. But too many secrets threaten their unexpected love. You can count on Helen to deliver a dramatic story filled with romance.

Don't forget to start your holiday shopping early this year. Our LOVESWEPT Golden Classics featuring our Hometown Hunk winners are out in stores right now, and in the beginning of November you can pick up our lovely December LOVE-SWEPTs. They make great gifts. What could be more joyful than bringing a little romance into someone's life?

Best wishes,
Sincerely,

Carolyn Nichols

Carolyn Nichols
　Editor
LOVESWEPT
Bantam Books
666 Fifth Avenue
New York, NY 10103

FAN OF THE MONTH

Tricia Smith

I'm honored to have been chosen as a "fan of the month" for LOVESWEPT. A mother of two children with a house full of animals, I've been a romance reader for years. I was immediately captivated when I read the first LOVESWEPT book, **HEAVEN'S PRICE** by Sandra Brown. Ms. Brown is a very compelling author, along with so many of the authors LOVESWEPT has introduced into my life.

Each month I find myself looking forward to new adventures in reading with LOVESWEPT. The story lines are up-to-date, very well researched, and totally enthralling. With such fantastic authors as Iris Johansen, Kay Hooper, Fayrene Preston, Kathleen Creighton, Joan Elliott Pickart, and Deborah Smith, I'm always enchanted, from cover to cover, month after month.

I recently joined the Gold Coast Chapter of Romance Writers of America and have made wonderful friends who are all well-known authors as well as just great people. I hope to attend an RWA convention someday soon in order to meet the authors who've enriched my life in so many ways. Romance reading for me is not a pasttime but a passion.